Runaway To Glory

Runaway To Glory

By Alice E. Christgau

WITH ILLUSTRATIONS BY

Leo R. Summers

NEW YORK: YOUNG SCOTT BOOKS

Acknowledgments

Grateful acknowledgment is hereby given to my brother, Walfred, for his oral and written "Memories of Grandpa" and his assistance with research on the Fourth Minnesota Regiment; and to my husband, Chris, for his steady encouragement and his patience in changing all those typewriter ribbons.

Contents

To The Memory Of My Mother

Selma Erickson

whose stories about Grandpa Sven usually concluded with the question: "Shouldn't such a thing
be written up?" thus providing the first inspiration
for the writing of this book.

1

What Makes A Grandpa?

Reuben wished it had not been such a perfect day for baseball. Missing recesses was bad enough any time, in any weather, but to have to stay in the schoolroom on a day that was warm and dry—just right in every way for baseball — that was almost unendurable. He pulled a library book out of his desk and settled down to read.

It was noon recess at Hay Lake School, District Number Two. The year was 1905, and it was the first week in May. Shouts of the older boys at their game of baseball behind the woodshed and the younger children playing pumpum-pullaway in the front schoolyard came through the open windows.

9

At the moment Reuben was feeling more rebellious than ever about having to miss all his recesses for another week. He sat quietly enough in his seat, but every now and then the anger he felt toward Miss Hibbard flared openly.

The whole thing had come about because of the Arbor Day program. Reuben was sure he would dislike Arbor Day all his life because of it, though of course he would still like trees as much as ever. Miss Hibbard had assigned him a long poem to memorize for the program. It was not that he minded learning it. He just did not like the idea of being the only boy having to stand up to speak while a bunch of girls went through a silly "planting a tree" pantomime. And he just couldn't see any sense in standing up and speaking a poem to a tree, no matter how much he liked trees. The idea struck him as plain foolishness.

So, by every means possible, he had tried to get out of it. He had offered to dig the hole

10

for the tree. He had said he would bring a bag of fertilizer from home all the way to school, certainly a smelly job. He had offered to play his cornet for the singing, even though he had a tendency to squeak on the high notes when he got the least bit flustered.

But Miss Hibbard had said *no* to everything. She had told him that he had the best speaking voice of all the older boys in her school and besides, he memorized easily. That was why she had chosen him to speak the "Tribute to Our Tree." If he wouldn't — well, she would have to get one of the girls to do it instead, but it would not be as effective. In fact, she would be most unhappy about it, for the piece was meant for a boy. And as for Reuben — well, he would simply have to lose all his recesses for two weeks. That was her usual punishment for insubordination. Without even looking up the long word, Reuben understood that it meant disobeying orders.

Miss Hibbard had looked him over coolly.

"You can think about it and take your choice," she had said, certain that he would choose to speak the piece instead of taking the "stay-in" penalty.

Well, Reuben had taken his choice; Arbor Day had come and gone, and here he was sitting at his desk in the empty schoolroom on a perfect spring day, with a game going on outside. It was Monday of the second week of his punishment. His whole being ached to be outdoors, to join in the game.

He tried to read, but found it hard to concentrate with happy shouts of "Strike three!" and "Fan him out!" floating in from outside.

Yet he knew that he could not honestly blame Miss Hibbard. After all, Teacher's word was law. If anyone chose to disobey, he had to be prepared to take the consequences. His own stubbornness had been part of it. He'd been scolded about this often at home, and had been told that it was something he'd have to get over.

Only Grandpa, who had been in the war and knew a lot about what was really important, had been at all understanding. He had told him that it was all right to be stubborn sometimes. "If you believe strongly in a thing, don't be ashamed to stand by it," he'd said. "Pay no mind to what anyone says if you feel inside yourself that you're right. People who have no convictions or nothing to be stubborn about seldom stand for very much of anything either, I've noticed. 'Long as you were willing to do other things for the program, you had a right to be a mite strong-willed. But I can see Miss Hibbard's side, too. In the army now, insubordination is a bad thing, for a soldier's life can depend on obeyin' orders, you know." Grandpa had slipped into his slurred, easy "war way" of talking, as he did when he warmed to reminiscences of his army days.

"I think I woulda spoke the piece and been done with it, if it'd been myself. Seems like bein' stubborn cost you more trouble than

14

speakin' the piece coulda done. But then if I'd been your teacher, I think I woulda let you get by too. Hard to say who's in the right, exactly, but it's that way with many things in life. You figger an' figger on some things, an' even then you can't allus be sure you come up with the right idee. Anyway, best thing now is take your punishment an' be as cheerful about the whole thing as you can."

That was exactly what Reuben was trying to do. He knew that anything Grandpa told him was sure to be right and true; his advice had never failed him yet. And, also as Grandpa had predicted, he had come to know and understand Miss Hibbard a little bit better during the missed recesses.

Though he sometimes disagreed with her, there were a lot of things about her that he liked. She was different from other teachers he had known. She was new in the community and knew little about some things, but there were other things that she seemed to understand better than most grown-ups he knew. Take the way he felt about Grandpa, for instance; he was sure that Miss Hibbard would understand that, because she had so much respect for the history of our country. And Grandpa—though most people seemed to have forgotten it—was a part of that history.

Sometimes when they were alone in the schoolroom they talked of things that you ordinarily would not discuss with a teacher. Miss Hibbard had told Reuben a great deal about her home state, West Virginia. She had lived there until her parents died. Then she had come north to Minnesota to live with an uncle who gave her a home and helped her through college. It was easy to see that she liked West Virginia better than Minnesota. She told Reuben that as soon as she had earned enough money to pay her uncle back for her education, she hoped to go "back east" again.

Today the conversation turned to Reuben's family—in particular, his grandfather. Their history lesson had been about General Sherman's campaign in the Civil War, and they had talked a great deal about his famous march "from Atlanta to the sea." Miss Hibbard had made such an interesting story out of it, especially when she talked of the Battle of Atlanta and the preparations for the march, that even the little first-graders had looked up from their coloring and busy work to listen.

When he came back to the schoolroom after lunch, Reuben announced casually to Miss Hibbard, correcting papers at her desk, "My Grandpa was with General Sherman in that march—all the way to Richmond. He saw the General a couple of times, and heard him speak once, too!" He could not keep a hint of pride out of his voice. He was, after all, the only boy in school who had a Union army veteran for his grandfather.

But Miss Hibbard looked bewildered. "Your grandfather!" she said. "I don't understand how — are you sure? Why, it's impossible!"

17

Reuben's coppery hair seemed to rise on his head like stiff bristles. His face flushed red under its sprinkling of freckles. He cleared his throat and answered stubbornly, "Well, he was! He's told me about it lots of times, and I guess he knows what he's talking about."

"But I just don't understand how he could be — in the war, I mean. . . ." Miss Hibbard, aware of her unfamiliarity with the people in the community, stopped uncertainly.

"I guess a lot of people don't, the way they act, anyway." Reuben spoke with irritation and anger. The truth was beginning to dawn on him that no one but himself, now that Grandma was dead, seemed to care about Grandpa at all! He had thought Miss Hibbard might understand and be different, but she seemed as bad as the rest of them.

He continued stubbornly, "He *is* a Civil War veteran, though, just the same. And he's had a very interesting life and been through a lot of dangers. *You* know about Sherman's march—you told us all those things just today. And Grandpa knows and understands ever so many other things too. He's just about the most — the greatest —" Sudden indignation welled up strongly and he could not find words to go on.

"Well, of course, he must be a grand old man, and he may have been in the Grand Army of the Republic and all that," said Miss Hibbard soothingly. "The thing that puzzles me is how he can be your grandfather! I'm just questioning the relationship, that's all."

She smiled, almost apologetically, and looked hopefully at Reuben. Would she ever get all these family relationships straight, she wondered. Reuben looked back at her crossly.

"Well, I've called him Grandpa as long as I can remember," he retorted. "And whenever we go places together he tells everyone 'This is my youngest grandson.' I should think he ought to know!"

Reuben subsided into a stubborn silence.

He couldn't really explain everything to Miss Hibbard because he didn't know the whole story too well himself. There probably was no use trying to tell her anything about Grandpa, either. His resentment against her flared suddenly. What made her think she knew so much, anyway? Talking like that just showed how little she knew and understood about everything in the district. And cheating him out of his recesses just because he wouldn't say an old poem! He propped his book high on the desk and slid down in his seat until all but the top of his head was hidden. The only sound was the buzz of voices outside, now and then rising to a crescendo of shouts and shrieks.

When she came to the end of a pile of papers, Miss Hibbard stopped and took off her glasses. She leaned back in her chair and rubbed a hand wearily across her eyes.

"That makes twenty-nine arithmetic papers I've corrected since lunch," she said conversationally. "It does get tiresome after a while."

Reuben spoke a low "Yes, ma'am," but continued to read. He stole a quick glance at her and decided with her nose-pincher glasses off, she looked much younger and quite pretty.

"Say, tell me," she continued, speaking as if she were really very much interested, "where does your grandfather live?"

Reuben answered briefly, barely glancing up. "With us — on the farm, of course. Our house is big; Papa built it that way on purpose so Grandpa and Grandma could live with us in two rooms of their own. But then Grandma died last year, so now he just uses one room and takes his meals with us."

Miss Hibbard looked more puzzled than ever. "But, Reuben," she said, "just the other day you were telling me that both your father and your mother were born in Sweden; that they left their homes and their parents there to come as immigrants to this country. Now you tell me your grandfather is here, was in the Civil War, and is living with you! That's what I can't quite understand."

"Well, it has something to do with my mother being married before," Reuben answered. "He isn't exactly what you call my 'whole' grandpa, I guess. But he lives with us, 'cause he and Grandma said long ago that they never wanted to leave that farm. It's the only home they'd ever known in this country. Nobody's ever exactly explained everything to me," he finished lamely.

It was just like Miss Hibbard to need everything spelled out to the last detail. Reuben found her habit of trying to set him straight very irritating sometimes. Just like that — by saying Grandpa could not really be his grandfather at all—she had confused him. But most of all he was cross with himself for not having cleared up everything so he could not be confused. He could have asked a few questions. But until now it just hadn't seemed important.

Two little girls came in crying; someone had

pushed them down. Their knees were skinned and bleeding, and it was necessary for Miss Hibbard to assemble bandages, a basin of water, and the bottle of arnica, soothing both their hurt emotions and their smarting wounds. The conversation ended abruptly.

Reuben turned back to his book still irritated. He was thinking to himself: "Just because her ancestors came to this country a long time ago — before the Revolution even — she's so proud and important about everything in history."

But as he thought a bit more about it, he could not help conceding, "Of course, she had a grandfather in the Civil War too — the one she calls 'my senator grandfather.' She can be proud of him all right, because he helped make West Virginia a state by itself when they wanted to stay in the Union instead of being in the Confederacy with the rest of Virginia. Yah, he was pretty important all right. But she might remember once in a while that we can have things to be proud of too, even if our families are kind of new in this country. Grandpa had something to do with history too!"

The bell pealed out suddenly, ending noon recess. In a few moments hot, red-faced children began trooping in, taking their seats noisily.

"I made a home run!" panted Joe as he went by Reuben on his way to his own seat.

"You were out at third — never touched base!" shouted Carl fiercely from across the aisle. "Cheater!"

"Quiet! Come to order! Take your seats!" Miss Hibbard rapped firmly on her desk with a ruler. Gradually the forty-odd children stopped their talking, snuffling, and scuffling, and settled down to afternoon lessons.

2

Grandpa Explains A Name

Whenever there were questions Reuben wanted answered, he always turned to his grandfather. It seldom occurred to him to look for Papa, who was always hard at work, usually in some distant field or woodland, too busy or too tired to answer any but routine farmwork questions.

Reuben's older brothers, Will and Johnny, were equally busy and worked just as hard. They had done men's work almost from childhood, and now they seemed to have forgotten what it meant to be boys. Sometimes it seemed to Reuben they had grown to be nearly as silent and stern as Papa. This was especially true during heavy work seasons.

Today Reuben hurried home from school, eager to talk to Grandpa. He walked quickly ahead of his seven-year-old twin sisters, Ellen and Emily. They had their heads together as usual, chattering busy little-girl plans about paper dolls, doll dresses, and tea parties in the attic. They looked like dolls themselves, and were almost treated as such by Papa and Mama, who adored them.

Reuben saw Johnny at work in the woodland pasture near the road. He was fixing fence, and Reuben came up from behind, surprising Johnny so that he was able to pull him down for a bit of playful wrestling.

"Stop it, you fool!" Johnny got up quickly and sucked angrily at a small scratch on his hand. "See what you made me do? Grow up, can't ya? Can't you see I have work to do? Pa wants this fence tight by sundown so we can leave the cows out. 'Long as you're no help around here, you'd better not be such a nuisance either!"

Reuben could think of nothing to say and turned away hastily. He walked on homeward, wondering just what he ought to be doing, since he was seldom entrusted with anything really important. There were times when he wondered just where he belonged in this family.

Grandpa was not in the yard or in his room, but Mama, churning butter in the cellar, told Reuben, "Why don't you try the apple orchard? The new apple trees came. . . ."

Reuben hurried out to the orchard and found the old man there. Though it was late in the afternoon he was busily employed setting out young sapling apple trees. He was planting them near the old trees that were beginning to show signs of dying. Papa had decided that it was time to replace a few of these, and Grandpa had eagerly volunteered to do the job.

"Seems good to be planting something again," he said, greeting Reuben cheerily. "I set this Duchess out way back in 'sixty-five I guess. Yup—same year I came back from the war it were. It's about done for now—split down the middle and dying inside. Still trying to bear fruit, though. Just look at them blossoms! But in another year or so, it'll have to come down altogether. By then, this seedling I've planted in its shade will have made a good start."

He patted the earth around the small tree firmly with his spade, and Reuben added another dipper of water to the mound. It seemed to Reuben that the young sapling was looking up to the old tree trustingly, as if already feeling its protection.

The two of them sat down on the split-off trunk to rest. Grandpa mopped his face with a huge red handkerchief. Beads of sweat streamed down his flushed cheeks. His legs, in shapeless woolen trousers, stuck out stiffly, reaching barely to the ground.

It was strange, Reuben thought, that Grand-

29

pa, who had once seemed so big—almost as big as Papa—now was only a little bigger than Reuben himself. Being almost twelve now, he had begun to grow rapidly.

The size similarity was a bond between them. But there was something more, a stronger tie that grew out of the needs of both, for each seemed to stand in a lone position in the family, needing a companion close at hand.

Reuben was sure he caused Grandpa plenty of worry — with his stubborn streak, for instance, which asserted itself in many ways, like refusing to wear enough warm clothing at times. Least bit of a cough would start Grandpa looking at him or fussing over him with worried concern.

And, of course, there were times when Grandpa tried Reuben's patience more than a little, too. For one thing, he was such a talker, and when he got off on some subjects he could get a bit boring. Reuben was sure this was one of the reasons other people treated him so carelessly. Grandpa would start out by telling you something you really wanted to know, but then he'd go on and on. You'd probably heard him tell the same thing a dozen times before, and if you didn't want to be mean and hurt his feelings you'd stay till he was through. It could get very tiresome. But this was not true very often; most of the time he was an interesting talker who had been through all kinds of experiences other people didn't even begin to know anything about. But that didn't seem to make any difference; they still acted the same way.

Reuben couldn't figure it out. Why should a man who had been a pioneer and lived among the Indians and traded with them—had even been a brave soldier in a very big war— now become a sort of nuisance just because he had got old? It was as if they wanted to take all that away from him. There was a kind of injustice about it that bothered Reuben.

Reuben had once heard Mr. Benson, a

neighbor, explain Grandpa to a new arrival in the neighborhood, a man who had seemed impressed with the old soldier.

"Ah, so old Sven got you to listen to him. I should've warned you. That long-winded old coot won't ever let anyone forget he was in the war. He can be a real nuisance sometimes." Mr. Benson gave a short, harsh laugh. "Take to your heels when you see him coming—that's my advice. It's the only way to keep him from getting to be a bother."

"This May sun is unnatural hot," said Grandpa, fanning himself with his bandanna. His shirt, loosened at the throat, revealed tightly buttoned red flannel underwear.

"I should think you would be hot, wearing your winter underwoolies!" said Reuben sympathetically. "Ugh, you must feel prickly!"

"Good for rheumatism to keep 'em on in warm weather." Grandpa spoke comfortably, reaching into his pocket for his pipe. "Best treatment there is for stiff joints—warm sweat.

You should have your warm underwear on, too, boy." He glanced disapprovingly at Reuben in a cotton shirt open at the throat, and wearing no shoes or stockings.

He began filling his pipe from a deerskin pouch that Reuben knew had once belonged to a Chippewa chieftain. "Your Mama don't like for me to smoke," he went on, glancing nervously at the house. "Says it's bad for my rheumatism and heart. But I had it—the rheumatism—long afore I began to smoke. Sleeping on the ground and wading through them rivers on the march is what did it. The chill got in my bones and stayed."

He puffed placidly as he sat studying the newly planted tree. Reuben, beside him, enjoyed the sensation of new grass pricking his bare feet.

"Miss Hibbard says that you aren't really my Grandpa at all," he began, plunging into the subject hastily. He wanted to get into it before Grandpa had a chance to enlarge on

33

the subject of his rheumatism, which had been unusually bad this spring. "I was telling her today how you'd been in Sherman's army and marched through Georgia, and she said she couldn't understand how you could be my grandfather, because, well—you know I have grandparents in Sweden, too. She's new here, of course."

The old man had been puffing easily and steadily and had seemed hardly to be listening, but now he took the pipe out of his mouth and began to speak. "Well, in a real legal way she's right, you know. I'm Will's and Johnny's grandpa, but not yours, legally speaking. But then no one pays any mind to legal ways of talking when it comes to home things simple as that.

"Still, maybe I ought to explain everything to you, in case you're a bit muddled about it. Your Mama doesn't want to talk about it—not that I blame her, mind—and your Papa's so busy with work by day and so tired evenings.

36

Someone should tell you the story. You're old enough to know, 'specially since the question's come up."

Grandpa looked off in the distance a moment and broke a small branch off the old apple tree to brush away the gnats that hung around his face. His pipe had gone out; he held it cradled in his hand as he began slowly to talk.

"You know, of course, that your Mama was married once before. Her first husband was my own dear son, John—Will and Johnny's father. Likely you had some knowing of this in the back of your mind though it was never talked of before."

Grandpa's voice had begun to tremble, but he went on bravely. "John, who was our only son, was killed in a logging accident in the north woods—an accident that never would have happened if the boss had taken just a little care to make the work safe. But—well, it happened when your Mama and him had been married only two years. Fifteen years ago it was last February."

Grandpa swept his bandanna over his face quickly. It looked suddenly pinched and pitiful, and his eyes were filled with tears. Mama had told Reuben that it was a sign of old age and decreasing strength that Grandpa cried so easily. She had warned that it was best not to get him thinking or talking about the old days. Reuben felt momentarily guilty, but he could think of no way to change the subject now.

After a few minutes Grandpa blew his nose hard and continued. He spoke quietly as if remembering out loud. "It's quite a long time ago, and Time heals all wounds, as they say. Well, Will and Johnny—such big, strong fellows now — they were babies then; in fact, Johnny wasn't even born till two months after his Pa was dead. It was a sad time for all of us, most of all for your Mama. I were younger then, but still I couldn't begin to do the farmwork alone, with my bad legs and all. Your Mama and me tried to do the outside work while Grandma stayed in looking after the little ones—it was a nigh-desperate situation.

"And then your Papa, a fine bachelor fellow and John's own best friend, he came forward and began to help your mother every way he could. Then he courted her and in time they got married and he took over. I blessed him for it. He built the new house, next to the log house we now call the summer kitchen, and made it big enough so Grandma and I could go on living there. It's his farm now. He's done real well too, being such a good worker. And he's been good to us, too. . . ."

In spite of the cheerful words, the sad look stayed on Grandpa's face. Reuben waited quietly, giving a discreet cough after a while to suggest that he was there, waiting for him to finish. Grandpa came back with a start.

"Where was I? Oh, yes—the farm. Well, I took this hundred-and-twenty-acre guv'ment claim back there in 'fifty-two. I had come, a young immigrant to this country, with but two dollars in my pocket. . . ."

Reuben could see a whole new train of thought starting. If Grandpa got going on his under-privileged boyhood in Sweden, he could go on and on a long time. Besides, he would be likely to remember more sad things.

"I can still call you Grandpa though, can't I?" he broke in earnestly. "Even if you aren't my real one—in a legal way like you said—I can still tell people that you're my Grandpa and all about how you fought in the war and marched with General Sherman and everything?"

"God bless you, yes!" Grandpa was once more his serene, contented self. He relit his pipe and blew a chain of smoke rings into the branches of the apple tree where they hung momentarily like garlands. He put his arm around Reuben's shoulders and gave him an affectionate hug.

"I'm your Grandpa, legal or no, and don't you pay no mind to what anyone else says on that! How would you get along otherwise, with both your grandfathers in Sweden—one of them already dead besides? But it's easy to see how your teacher got mixed up when you'd told her both your parents came from Sweden, leaving homes and families there."

He studied the ground intently for a few moments, repeating some words softly to himself. "You know I think I like that name best in English." He said "Grandfather" and "Grandpa" slowly to himself and listened as if hearing them for the first time. "As a boy in Sweden, I was taught to say 'Farfar' or 'Morfar' to my grandfathers. But those names only say that a man is the father of your father or the father of your mother. They don't really have any other meaning.

"But 'Grandfather' now—that really means something! That explains what a man should be to his grandchildren. I don't rightly know what that book, the one you find meanings of words in—the dictionary—what it says about the meaning of the word 'grand.' But to me it just means something extra good. And that's what a Grandpa should be — an extra good Papa! The way I see it, every boy needs one close by, what with parents so busy and all...."

"That's just it," Reuben broke in eagerly. "I knew all the time you weren't exactly my *whole* Grandpa, but I couldn't exactly explain it. And I never thought much about it before. But the way Miss Hibbard talked, as if, well...."

"She doesn't understand all these things, you see, not having lived here long," said Grandpa peaceably. "But don't you pay no mind to what anyone says on that subject no more."

"Pay no mind"—the expression that seemed to belong to Grandpa alone—fell like balm on Reuben's ears. Grandpa had explained once that it was one he'd picked up from Yankee soldier companions in the war. "I've forgotten much of that talk," he had said. "Don't know just why that particular expression stays by me. Must be it's an extra good one."

Reuben was sure that it was. Anyway, whenever he heard it, he was greatly comforted. If a man who had lived such a full and dangerous life as Grandpa could say that a thing was not worth minding, it very likely was not worth worrying about.

Grandpa stood up and shouldered the spade. "Time to get back to the house," he said. "Your Mama may have something she wants you to do afore supper."

They started to walk back, skirting the edge of a field where Will was riding the disk harrow. Though not yet seventeen, he was already doing a man's work on the farm. He waved to them to wait as he came riding up to the end of the field. The earth gleamed dark and moist behind him; only a narrow strip of hard brown soil still remained to be harrowed

43

before the field would be ready for corn planting.

Will pulled the horses to a stop. He looked hot and angry. "Tell Ma to get some warm water and bandages ready. I'll be needing some fixing up when I finish," he said shortly. "Hurt my hand on one of the disks, pulling out quack grass. Nasty cuts. . . ." He held out his hand, showing lacerated, bleeding skin.

"Let me finish that little piece for you," said Grandpa. "That hand should be washed and tended to — bandaged with arnica and salve soon as possible, and it'll take at least an hour to finish up the field."

Will's answer was almost scornful. "Naw," he said. "I'll finish. You might have a runaway again, like the last time I let you take over the reins." He smacked the backs of the horses briskly and drove on in a cloud of dust.

Grandpa's face looked like the face of a child who had just been slapped. Reuben felt he was seeing his own face again that day last

44

week when he forgot and left the gate open and the cows got out.

"Can't you even learn enough responsibility to close a gate after you?" Papa had asked witheringly, not even waiting for an explanation. Reuben, washing his hands at the sink, had just stood there staring at his reflection in the mirror over the sink. He remembered the sort of crumpled, ready-to-cry look on his face.

Grandpa's face looked like that now, but all he said was, "I'll put the spade away. You run and tell your Mama to get the things ready for Will."

3

"Grandpa Is Too Old!"

Grandpa did not come to the table for supper. He explained to Mama that he felt "a bit done in, with the hot sun and the planting," and would be glad just to have a bit of bread and milk in his room. Reuben brought it to him, being careful to include a generous portion of the dessert, rice pudding with raisins.

At the supper table later, everyone ate hungrily and silently for a while. Then Papa buttered a piece of bread with extra care and cleared his throat, a signal that he had something to announce. Everyone waited expectantly, continuing to eat as quietly as possible.

Finally he spoke: "We'll be needing more seed corn so that we can finish planting in the next few days. Can't take the time to go after it myself." He looked at Will with some concern. "From the looks of that hand you'd better stay around here tomorrow and keep soaking it off and on or you're likely to get an infection there. We're real short-handed, and that's the truth."

Johnny looked up questioningly, but Papa went on: "I can't spare you, either. There's the forty across the road still to be disked, and the corn planters to get in shape. Everything's just right for planting now—fields neither too wet nor too dry. I want to get in the corn—the sooner the better. So I must have that seed right away."

Reuben held his breath. Would he be the one chosen to go? He had been allowed to drive Dolly with the buggy, once to Marine and once to Scandia Center, but this evidently was to be a much longer trip, most likely to Stillwater.

Boys could be kept home from school during busy seasons on a farm. Reuben went on eating, but his face was flushed with eager hopefulness. Papa looked at him suddenly and for a few moments sat studying him.

"Do you think Mama and you could manage a trip to Stillwater together? She'd do the driving, of course. But you'd be along to take care of hitching up, loading the sacks, and things like that. You'll have to take the team and the spring wagon. It's a fair trip."

A too-quickly swallowed mouthful of scalloped potatoes burned all the way down Reuben's throat and lay, a hot lump, in his chest.

"Sure," he said, rubbing his chest hard to relieve the burning inside. "Sure — we can manage fine."

But Mama was looking doubtful. "I've been thinking it over," she said, "And really, I don't see how I can take the time. It would mean a whole day, and I have those new chicks on my hands. If I don't see to them every three hours or so they crowd in the brooder house and die—as they did last year. And I should be getting the garden in too, and doing some house-cleaning, and sewing for the girls. There just isn't time for everything I have to do in the spring."

She smiled wistfully. "Not but what I wouldn't enjoy the trip. I haven't been to Stillwater in over a year, and I need a new hat and some other things. There are such good stores there, too."

Papa looked troubled and uncertain. It appeared that he would have to take time off and go himself. He seemed considering this silently.

Reuben looked up and spoke quickly. "Why can't Grandpa go with me? He could do the driving—he knows the way and everything."

Papa frowned and went on eating. "I just don't think he can be trusted any more," he said after a moment. "Oh, maybe 'trusted' isn't the right word—but you know what I mean. The team is strong and frisky, and he's too old.

49

He's acting real feeble lately, I've noticed;
seems all he can do is talk, talk, talk. . . ."

"But that's because he doesn't have anything really important to do!" Reuben spoke
hotly. "He planted the little apple trees this
afternoon just fine. I was there and saw how
good he'd done it! He needs—"

Everyone had stopped eating to look at him.
He began to eat again, hurriedly bolting his
food.

"Anyone can see he's failing," said Mama
soothingly. "It isn't his fault he's old. I doubt
he could get up in the spring wagon even. His
rheumatism has been worse than usual this
spring."

"I could help him with that—climbing up,
I mean—and anything else, too," said Reuben
stoutly. He felt suddenly defensive and angry.
"Seems like no one will hardly give him credit
for anything any more. You'd think he wasn't
even a man—and he's been a soldier and everything! Why should everyone forget all the

good things about a person just 'cause he's getting old?"

Will looked witheringly at Reuben. "Seems like you forget a few things yourself! How about the runaway he had with the hayrack last fall? I haven't forgotten that; got a broken arm out of it that still aches sometimes." He stroked his left arm with his recently bandaged right hand. Everyone looked sympathetic, and Reuben felt uncomfortably alone against them all.

"But you said yourself that day the horses were scared by the automobile coming up suddenly from behind and honking. You were right there and saw it," he finished doggedly.

"Yeah, and I saw that Gramp was busy talking to the mail carrier instead of holding tight to the reins and tending to business like he should've been!" Will pushed back his chair and got up to leave.

"Hush your arguing, you two!" said Papa sternly. He remembered all too well the accident that had broken Will's arm and wrecked the hayrack — all because of a few minutes' chat with the reins lying slack.

Still, such a situation would not likely arise on this trip. Reuben was getting to be pretty dependable, except for a lapse now and then. And maybe the boy was right; maybe the old man needed to feel useful, especially at busy times like this.

Papa laid down his knife and fork in a precise X across his empty plate. He studied the table a few moments, then looked over at Reuben and smiled slightly.

"Well, say I let him try driving the team again. And say I give you the chance to show me you're a big enough boy now to take some responsibility too. Will you see that he tends to business the whole time and doesn't get into any trouble — like stopping along the road to talk, or spending too much time with that crony of his at the Soldiers' Home? He takes a good bit of managing, you know."

"I sure will!" Reuben answered quickly. "We'll manage fine together. You'll see!"

He felt eager and elated, for he had won a double victory. He was entrusted with the responsibility of a trip to Stillwater, and though Papa did not put it that way, it was a joint responsibility with Grandpa. And he was the one who had won it for them both.

A Trip Into Danger

And so, because of the necessary trip, Reuben missed both his school classes and the stay-in punishment the following day. New as she was to the community, Miss Hibbard understood that at times urgent farmwork or errands came before school attendance.

Papa gave final instructions about the seed corn—where it was to be bought, exactly what kind, and how many bushels. He showed Reuben how to handle the sacks and where to stow them in the wagon. He gave Grandpa money to pay for everything. He warned that as they approached Stillwater they would be likely to meet some of the new motorcars, and instructed him on handling the horses in such

54

encounters. He explained also where to go to water the horses, and how important it was not to water them until they were cooled off, as it might bring on colic. All these things Grandpa knew before, but he listened patiently, nodding his head now and then to show his complete understanding.

Then came a few last admonitions. "And if you must go to the Old Soldiers' Home to see Gus, don't stop over long. Have a cup of coffee with him, but let Reuben wait outside with the horses. That way you won't sit so long maybe—if you know he's holding the horses. You should start for home by four at the latest. Remember to hold the horses in, coming home. They'll be hungry by that time and a little wild unless they feel strong hands on the reins."

Grandpa, already seated in the spring wagon, nodded briskly and gave an authoritative tug to the reins. "Don't worry, Alfred," he said easily. "I guess I can still handle a team.

The trouble is in my legs, you know. We'll make out fine. Why, once I drove to Stillwater early in March—back in 'eighty-six, I b'lieve it were—and got caught by a turrible blizzard right there in the tamarack swamp. It seemed like dusk at mid-afternoon—the air so thick with whirling snow. And the horses—oh, my, they were all confused and could hardly go against that wind, you know. But I managed. . . ."

He stopped, for Papa had turned away. He was on the porch speaking softly to Reuben, who was squirming under his mother's final swipe with a washrag. He buttoned his jacket and pulled manfully at his bow tie as he listened to the familiar admonitions: "Remember he's old. Take charge and manage him as much as possible. You're almost twelve now—getting to be a man, or should be. Today you must be one."

Reuben felt a small twinge of worry. All this harping on Grandpa's age and his weak-

ness—maybe there was something to it, after all. But he hastily brushed the thought aside.

"Don't you worry," he said confidently. "Nothing will go wrong. We'll get along fine, and we'll be home in plenty of time too."

Mama brought out the basket of lunch and carefully placed it in the bottom of the wagon between their feet. Papa tucked the fringed carriage robe around their knees and adjusted a girth strap. Grandpa settled his black felt hat firmly on his head, then, slackening his hold on the reins, spoke a firm "Gidyup!" to the waiting horses, who had been stamping impatiently ever since they were put in harness.

Here and there in the road were patches of mud that made heavy going for the wagon. But the sprightly blacks managed to keep a steady trot. Not having had much exercise since the spring thaw had put an end to sleigh travel, they seemed eager to run.

Reuben thought he knew just how they felt.

After the confinement of his days at school without recess, he felt suddenly joyous and free. It was going to be a wonderful day!

Grandpa and he sat silent for a while, savoring the exciting adventure of the trip. Grandpa looked straight ahead and was completely taken up with the business of driving.

Reuben sniffed delightedly the odors his nose encountered. Even the morning air itself was fresh and sweet as if newly washed. He could hardly get enough of it and kept inhaling deeply. Now and then the perfume of early plum and cherry blossoms also greeted his nostrils as they passed the slender trees along the road. They reminded Reuben of girls in billowy, white dresses.

And there was a different kind of smell—sweet, but with a kind of tang to it. It was from freshly flowing sap of willow, maple, alder, and hazelwood bushes. All these odors blended together into one delicious aroma that meant only one thing—spring.

Even the strong smell of the horses was good. It was rank and heavy, mingling with the smell of warm leather in the wagon seats. Reuben had been around horses ever since he could remember, even though he was seldom allowed to drive them. Today their smell suggested only one thing — grown-up strength. Papa had told him he was almost a man. Letting him make this trip showed that he really meant it.

But it was going to be a long drive to Stillwater. The last admonitions still rang in Reuben's ears and he wondered how he could best keep the trip going smoothly, just in case. . . . He wondered if it might not be a good idea to get Grandpa telling some of his favorite stories. That way he wouldn't feel any particular need to stop and talk if they should happen to meet someone they knew.

Of course, he had heard most of the stories before, and, well—there were times when anyone might find the repetition tiresome. But

now that his history class was on the subject
of Sherman's march, Reuben thought he might
not mind hearing some of those things over
again. Grandpa did know a few extra things
about General Sherman, things that weren't
in the history books.

Neighbors, and even Papa and Will and
Johnny, would smile in a weary, bored sort of
way when Grandpa began a war story, letting
you know that they'd heard it before and
would just as soon he'd skip the telling. But
the worst was when they would simply get up
and walk away from him when he was right
in the midst of it, leaving him standing alone,
flustered and foolish-looking, apparently talking to himself.

It was not only when Grandpa was telling
old stories either. Just two weeks or so ago,
Constable Campbell had stopped in to water
his horse and to talk with Papa about the bank
robbery in Scandia Center. It had occurred
the day before, and since Papa had been in

town that day, the constable wondered if he had noticed anything unusual or suspicious.

But though Papa had transacted business as usual both at the bank and in the store, he had seen nothing out of the way, and told the constable so. They agreed that it was a mysterious and even shocking thing. Bank robberies had been occurring in other places for years, but none had ever come that close before.

Grandpa had been listening from the porch, and suddenly he spoke up, rather hesitantly, as if trying to remember. He had been along to town and he explained that something happened just as he was going into the general store that, now he thought about it, seemed mighty strange. Across the road from the store was the cemetery hedge, and near it he'd heard a couple of voices talking together.

"They were strange to me," he said, "and struck me because one was so deep and sounded sorta ugly, like a man with a mean temper, and the other was as high-pitched as a woman's almost, and seemed to come from a reasonable kind of man, trying to get along. . . .

"As I was saying, they were new to me, those voices, so when I came to the top of the store steps I turned around, slow-like to see who they were. Well, when I got myself turned around—'count of my rheumatism I'm slow, you know — why there was no one there! Looked like they stepped behind the hedge or something to hide—on purpose! That struck me as sort of funny, you know. Why should anyone want to hide from me? But I really didn't pay it much mind until now. Somehow it sort of figgers in with what you were saying."

"If you did'na see anyone, you may as well save your-r br-reath!" The constable had turned away impatiently. And Papa, too, had looked impatient as if he wished Grandpa would leave him and Mr. Campbell alone. It was not often that he was honored with such a visit.

Grandpa had turned away and stumped into the house. He looked like a little boy who had been rebuked for being "mouthy." Even though he seemed to understand now that no one cared to listen to him for long on any subject at all any more, it appeared that the knowledge still hurt.

The blacks kept up their tireless trotting and they were passing the schoolyard now. It was "school-time" so there was no one outside to witness Reuben's proud flashing by. He wished it might have been morning recess when the other boys would have been out behind the woodshed playing baseball.

His thoughts turned again to his lost recesses and to Miss Hibbard. Unfair as the punishment seemed, he had to admit that she was quite fair in other ways. She had shown more than once that she appreciated people like Grandpa; it came out when she taught history especially. Some things about her made Reuben and the other big boys just plain mad.

64

She had too many programs, causing such trouble as the Arbor Day piece. But in other ways—well, Reuben bet she wasn't like some people who didn't even have sense enough to appreciate an old soldier. This was a good chance to ask Grandpa a few things; then tomorrow he'd have more to tell her than just that business about how they were related.

"Yesterday in history we studied about the Battle of Atlanta and about Sherman's march," Reuben began, settling himself more comfortably in the wagon seat. "Miss Hibbard said Sherman's men were called 'bummers' for a good reason, but I argued with her about that. I told her that you'd explained the real bummers were a kind of raggle-taggle bunch of hoboes that followed the army, or went ahead of it, just taking advantage of the war and Sherman's name so they could loot and steal. You told me once that they were not the same thing as the army foragers who were under orders to bring in food for the army and the horses. Well, anyway, Miss Hibbard said she guessed she'd have to admit that Sherman was quite a brilliant general all right. She said he might come next to Grant—even to George Washington! Do you think so?"

Grandpa sat up a bit in the seat, looking straight ahead at the road. His hands held the reins firmly, and he looked neither feeble nor old now. A sort of "soldier look" had come into his eyes, a look that Reuben had observed before whenever their conversation turned to the war.

"Well, now, I would cert'nly say 'yes' to that," he answered sagely. "I think I'd even put Uncle Billy ahead of both of 'em. We called General Sherman that, you know, 'cause he was more like an uncle to his men than a commander. The word was, he felt such concern he hardly slept nights for figgerin' out how to keep his men from gettin' killed.

" 'Course, it's always hard to compare generals when they was in different wars. Still and all, I think I'd have to say Uncle Billy was the greatest in all American history, if I was to really put my mind to decidin' between 'em. It's outsmartin' the other side that shows who's really the best. And Uncle Billy, he were a genius at that."

Reuben was delighted to hear Grandpa fall into his careless, slurring way of talking again. It was what Grandpa called his "Yankee way of talk" and it meant that he had slipped back into the war years, and was reliving army experiences of more than forty years before.

Reuben tried to speak sagely too, to measure his book knowledge of the war against Grandpa's real life experiences of it.

"Well, of course, I know it was awfully clever the way he kept dodging around and fooling the Reb generals so they never knew where he was going to turn up. They said even President Lincoln didn't really know what he was up to. When someone asked about General Sherman, he said, 'I know where he went in at, but I don't know where he's coming out at.' "

"That's it!" Grandpa chortled gleefully. "Warn't that smart of him now? And all the time we was destroyin' the railroads and cuttin' off Reb army supplies, and movin' steadily to unite forces with Grant—without once fightin' a real battle. They called us 'The Lost Army' you know, but we was never lost, not for a minute. Oh, Uncle Billy had it all figgered out from the beginning—how best to keep 'em guessin'.'"

Reuben tried to look judicious, as if he were regularly in the habit of appraising plans and strategies of army generals.

"What I'm wondering, though," he began slowly, "was it the best way to do it? Causing so much destruction of property, and making those people in Georgia and South Carolina so awful mad, I mean. Maybe it would have been better if he'd met their armies and fought battles instead."

Grandpa looked suddenly stern. "It were the best way. Take my word for that, son. It saved lives! That's what Uncle Billy tried to do, and other generals up to that time hadn't bothered about so much. Until Sherman came along, no one had really faced up to what war was. You might say he was the general that changed the whole idea of war. Until then it had always been a kind of game, cruel and turrible, but with a kind of glory to it. In battles, one side was the winner and the other almost all killed off—just one big battlefield duel after another until one side plumb wore out or had lost too many men to go on.

"But that didn't make sense to Cump Sherman—no-siree. He set out to change the idee. He explained that the way to decide a war was not all by fightin' and killin,' but by the *movement of troops.* He said he only wanted to conquer the South, not kill 'em off. You have to admit that was better than the other way. And besides, it worked!"

69

"That's probably why you're alive today and able to tell about it," said Reuben admiringly. "Even with your bad rheumatism, you're much better off than if you'd been killed or badly wounded."

"That's right, boy. A bit of grapeshot hit me in the knee afore we took Savannah; I guess you know about that. It's the reason I was in a hospital there for a while, though I was able to take up the march into South Carolina with the rest of 'em, 'cause we stayed so long in Savannah. Crossing icy rivers, with water up to our armpits, that weren't easy with a stiff knee. The rheumatism started about then. But the thing we all feared most was gettin' into one of those turrible prisons. Why, you hardly had a chance to come out alive if you were wounded and got captured. The wounded gets the worst of battles, Uncle Billy said; that's why, as much as possible, he kept his men from havin' to fight pitched battles."

70

Grandpa flicked a bee off Ned's back with an expert flip of the whip and drove carefully through a muddy patch.

"Don't ever doubt that the way Sherman did it were the best way," he continued. "The march saved a lot of lives and finished up the war. And it could have stopped sooner if the Reb generals had given up sooner. They knew they was licked when we took Atlanta, but they was plumb stubborn. Uncle Billy had to bring home to 'em what a bad thing war is, and what a mistake they'd made tryin' to bust up the country. It was South Carolina started it, you know."

"Yes, I know," Reuben spoke almost apologetically. "But Miss Hibbard says — even though she admits he was a very smart general and all that—she says General Sherman was awful rough and hard. Seems as though the southern states have never been able to forgive the Union army for that march."

"True, true. They hated us bad." Grandpa

71

gave a mournful chuckle. "Even though they knew it was mostly the raggle-taggle follerin' us that they feared most. They begged Sherman for protection from them! And those were often their own people.

"But I got called a 'bummer' more'n once myself, and I learned to pay it no mind, nor any of the hard words spoke to us. Boy, we was in a war! You know we couldn't have made that march without havin' to forage around the countryside for food. We had to get it off the land, or neither we nor our horses could have kept goin'.

"I ain't sayin' some things didn't happen, from the army too, at times. Remember, you're always bound to have some galoots along, such as won't obey orders and are out to get things for themselves, even in war. They get away with behavior they never would in peacetime. But Uncle Billy shouldn't be held to blame for that. He laid down plenty of rules, stiff ones too."

74

Grandpa had slowed the horses to meet an oncoming rig. "How are you, Sven?" It was the mail carrier, who seemed inclined to stop and chat. "Nice day, isn't it? Where you off to so early?"

Grandpa returned the greeting with dignity, but kept the horses to a brisk, steady walk. "Corn plantin' time; we're goin' after seed corn." He threw the information out without turning his head.

"I sure want to hear more about those rules," Reuben said, "so I can tell Miss Hibbard. She never said anything about rules for foragers, and the history books didn't either. It sounded as though the Union army just marched on and plundered right and left as they pleased."

"Well, they can't put everything in the history books, you know." Grandpa spoke placidly and reasonably. "There was just too much history bein' made there at one time. But we had rules. Oh my, yes! Don't you ever fergit it! We had rules about how to go after food and supplies, and what could be taken and what was not to be touched. Gus, my sergeant that we'll be seein' today, stood guard at many a front door, same time I stood at the back, to keep the men from enterin' the house and scaring women and children. At the same time, the foraging party would be out in the fields gettin' corn, potatoes, squash and such stuff, while others would be drivin' off hogs or cattle—all of it food and supplies we needed to keep goin'. We started from Atlanta with a three-days' supply of food, you know. After that it was up to us to get it off the land—or starve.

"I don't say nothing ever happened. Now and then there were some galoots who sneaked around and took clothes or family silver, valuable things or such like. But in our outfit, if they was caught, they got punished. I saw it more'n once."

"But what about the people, the ones you were steal—, I mean *taking* the stuff from?

Did they have anything left for themselves?"

"Most of the people had already run off. Here and there we would find stock left without food and water—some already dead. Oh, there were some sights sad to see. You were about to say 'stealing' just then. Well, in a way, I suppose it could be called that. In peacetime it would be."

He looked down at his hands and seemed to be studying them intently. "Yes, these hands had to do it sometimes, I'll admit. But in a war you do what you're told to do, if you think it right or not. Other lives than your own may depend on it. Uncle Billy were in command an' he had to keep us goin' an' help us survive enough to finish what we'd started. He was savin' us—an' the South too—from something much worse. Do you see?"

"Well, of course, anyone can see that it's different from—well, bank robbing." Reuben tried to speak judiciously. "Even Miss Hibbard, though she's kind of down on Sherman, still she admits that what he did could be justified if it was only to end the war. She was telling, though, that some of her relatives —a great-uncle, I guess, that lived near Savannah with his family—they had their plantation stripped of just about everything, and almost starved that winter."

Grandpa nodded sadly. "It figgers," he said. "Some of them plantations was hit hard. But if they suffered from hunger, anyway that was better than more killin' woulda been. And remember this — those that didn't resist our army was seldom hurt or even left destitute. They had to give up some of their crops and such, sure. But the rules said: 'You are to make no unreasonable demands.' Those were the exact words; I remember them well. Why we couldn't even fire our guns except at 'armed assailants.' We were fined fifty cents for every cartridge we couldn't give a good reason for firin'!"

They were passing a small tumbledown

barn with an equally dilapidated house near it. Grandpa looked hard at the forlorn-looking place and pointed with his whip. "Now a place like that—why, when our advance scouts came to anything so poor, they would just pass it by. No one who was already havin' trouble makin' out was to be bothered in any way. It may have happened now and then, but it was against orders. Of course, when it did, it got remembered. It's allus the bad things that's never forgot."

Grandpa looked off in the distance for several moments. When he spoke again, it was in an almost reverent tone of voice, as if his thoughts were on someone for whom he had a great and abiding admiration.

"I can tell you 'bout one time that proves we weren't out only for meanness, anyway. See, some of the real bummers had been ahead of us then and had gone over the farm of this poor widow woman, leavin' her nothin' for herself and her children but a few potatoes in her garden and a bit of meal in the house. Our captain heard about it, though Gus said it was someone much higher up that give the order. McClellan, he said, or even Uncle Billy himself. Anyway, next morning, two soldiers was sent back to her place with a mule cart loaded with corn, turnips, squash, and a few chickens. Behind the cart was tied a good big milk cow! Orders was to deliver it all to the widow's place, two miles to the rear. It were done too. I can tell you that for true, boy," Grandpa concluded with fierce earnestness. "I know, for I were one of them two soldiers!"

5

A Motorcar Ride At Last!

They had already passed through the village of Marine and were getting close to Stillwater now. Grandpa's attention was taken up with driving. He sat up very straight and erect and it was clear that he had stopped wartime reminiscences for the time being. The road between the little town of Marine and Stillwater was almost crowded with spring wagons and buggies. Here and there a light two-wheeled sulky whirled along behind a swift pacing horse, making all the other horses appear slow and heavy.

Quite suddenly a motorcar loomed up ahead, coming toward them rapidly. It flew forward enveloped in a cloud of dust and smoke, scattering sand and pebbles viciously in the horses' faces.

Grandpa yelled "Whoa!" and stopped the team at the far side of the road. He held tightly to the reins as they clung precariously on the edge of the ditch until the automobile had passed.

"No use gettin' mixed up with one of them jessie rigs," he said irritably. "What business they got on the roads anyway? Scarin' the horses like they do! There ought to be a law agin' them!"

Reuben smiled quietly to himself. In this matter he was not of the same mind as Grandpa—not at all. He accepted most of the old man's opinions as sound and true, but in the matter of the automobile, it was plain that Grandpa was both unreasonable and prejudiced. Reuben believed quite simply that the auto was a great invention and that it was here to stay.

He longed for a ride in even a small motorcar, but so far there had not been the slightest opportunity. Still, he hoped that the chance would come one day. More and more cars were appearing each year, even on remote country roads. One of these days, Reuben was sure he would be offered a ride in one.

Grandpa pulled up to the hitching post in front of Orrin's General Store. Reuben carefully helped him down, a difficult business since Grandpa's knees were very stiff and he was heavy. Grandma had once told Reuben that even though Grandpa had not been seriously wounded, he was a war casualty all the same. Those many nights of sleeping out in the open on the frozen ground had been too much for a man of his age. He had never really recovered from the ordeal.

The seed corn transaction was soon made. Reuben loaded the sacks into the wagon and stashed the groceries Mama had ordered under the seat. Their business was accomplished by noon, and they both felt like boys on a holiday with so much time left to spend as they liked.

First they decided to eat their lunch. They settled themselves under a tree at the back of the store and opened the big basket. They eagerly attacked the big rye bread sandwiches and hard-boiled eggs. With them, they ate two dill pickles just bought in the store. At the last they divided a nickel's worth of candy, licorice and peppermints, and refreshed themselves with two juicy oranges from the bag just bought. It was a perfect lunch.

After a while Grandpa took out his large turnip watch and studied it carefully. He got to his feet, looking busy and purposeful. "Now then," he said, "it's time we give the horses their drink at the trough on Main Street. And then I want to stop and visit with Gus for a spell. He would take it ill if I didn't stop just a bit to talk over old times. With his one leg, he don't get about as much as I do. He's prob'ly right lonesome."

Reuben was remembering Papa's admonition. He put in carefully, "I'll stay outside and hold the horses while you go in and have your visit. You know we're supposed to start home by four."

"We will, never fear," Grandpa answered easily. "Plenty of time for everything."

All would have gone as planned except that a brand new automobile, a saucy red two-seater with brass trimmings and white-spoked wheels, was standing in the driveway of the Old Soldiers' Home when they drove up. It was the most gorgeous motorcar that Reuben had ever seen, even in pictures. At its wheel sat a young man, nattily dressed in a deep visor cap of green and a long dust coat of the same color. He looked handsome and exactly right as the driver of such a perfect mechanical creation.

Old Gus Shottler was coming through the front door, wearing a long grey raincoat and a visor cap pulled down tightly over his ears.

86

It looked odd on such a warm day, but it was apparent that he had dressed that way because he thought it was appropriate for an automobile ride. He was looking expectantly at the car and hardly noticed the horse-drawn rig.

Grandpa was having difficulty subduing the horses. They skirted the strange contraption warily, as if expecting it to rise up and attack them. When they were at last quieted, Grandpa shouted a greeting at Gus.

Gus leaned on a crutch with his left arm and raised his hand in playful salute, which Grandpa returned with an impish smile. Reuben noticed how eager Grandpa's face had become. He shouted to no one in particular, "Pay him no mind, men! He's only a pore buck sergeant who got left in Uncle Billy's great army by mistake."

With equal playfulness, Gus retorted, "To your station, Corporal! Just who do you think is supposed to give orders in this here war?"

Grandpa handed the reins to Reuben and

scrambled down from the wagon, entirely without help. He stood pumping Gus's free hand and looking up into his face affectionately.

"Good to see you, Gus! Good to see you! My, you're lookin' good!" He turned and pointed at Reuben. "You know my youngest grandson, Reuben. He and I are down for seed corn today. We had a fine trip, and now that we have a little time, I thought we'd have a good visit together afore we have to start for home."

He had been talking breezily, but grew suddenly serious, looking at the automobile. "Who is that in the new ottymobile? A friend of yourn?"

Gus answered with hearty pride. "This is my nephew, Henry, and his new Oldsmobile. You've come just in time to go for a ride with us. Henry comes by every week to give me a ride; it's something I really look forward to now, more than anything else. He has one of

the first machines in town. You can't believe
how nice it rides!"

Henry turned and nodded carelessly from
the richly upholstered leather seat. Reuben,
sitting in the wagon holding the reins, looked
at him with wistful longing. He thought he
had never seen anyone who looked so completely sporting.

He tried to imagine the thrill of getting in
and driving off in that marvelous mechanical
creation. Think of the ease of just getting in
and starting without having to harness or hitch
up—not to mention feeding, watering, curry-
ing, and cleaning stalls. All the business that
went with driving a team seemed suddenly
hopelessly dull and stupid, though up until
now he had always been proud to be entrusted
with the care of the horses.

Already Ned and Fanny were becoming
restive. It was plain that they wanted to get
home to their stalls, to measures of oats and
mangers full of hay. Reuben held onto the

reins firmly, but it no longer seemed such an important responsibility to sit there and hold the horses. His eyes were fixed on the automobile.

"There's room in the back for my friend, Sven, and the boy, wouldn't you say, Henry?" Gus was slowly but definitely hobbling out toward the car. When he reached it he stepped in. It was a difficult maneuver with the crutch, but he had learned to manage it with skill.

Henry opened the back door invitingly. "Sure," he said cordially. "Come on—get in. The machine won't bite you!"

"We take a ride instead of sit on the porch and drink coffee today, eh?" Gus urged coaxingly from the front seat. "I hate to lose my chance for a ride; Henry won't come by again till next week. And we've walked plenty in our time, Sven. Now our walking days are over. So just tie up the horses there and come along. Take a ride in style!"

Reuben's heart was almost bursting with

91

desire. Here was the chance he had been waiting for! A chance to ride in such a beauty of an automobile as he had never even dreamed of! But he made himself remember Papa's words: "Don't tie up the horses. Start for home by four."

He looked at Grandpa hopefully. If he chose to go — on the proper conditions, of course, like being back on time — would he, Reuben, really be disobeying orders?

"Papa warned me about the driving — to make sure we didn't stop on the way, and to get started home on time. He didn't really say anything about in between. I bet he'd take the chance himself if he got it! Just the other day he said he'd like to see for himself if motorcars were so much easier to ride in."

It was obvious that Grandpa, too, had begun to waver. He looked at his watch and remarked to no one in particular that it was nearly three o'clock, more than an hour until they had to go. Of course, he had no use for the noisy contraptions, but if Gus insisted. . . . He thought a lot of Gus and would hate to miss the usual visit. There could be no harm in seeing what it was like to ride in a motorcar, then he'd know what it was about them that scared the horses. He looked at his watch again. If they went for just a short ride—say if Henry could have them back here in less than an hour?

Gus looked at Henry earnestly. "Any time you say," Henry said easily. "I make fifteen miles an hour on country roads. You wanted to go out the river road today and look down on Log Jam Point. Plenty of time for that."

"We'll come," said Grandpa with sudden eagerness. He hurried over to the hitching post and began to tie up the horses.

"Wind the reins around the whipstock and come down," he said to Reuben. "I never thought I'd be riding in one of them rigs in my lifetime, but like Gus says, we have walked a bit in our time. No harm now to try any new way of riding we can. I would hate to go back

93

without a little visit—hard to say when I'll get down here again. And the river road and Log Jam Point—I haven't been there in years!"

Reuben did as he was told without further thought. He scrambled down and ran to the automobile.

Grandpa had already climbed in and was sitting in the back seat, chatting happily with the men in front. Reuben slid into the luxurious leather seat. Henry slammed the door shut with the air of a man about to give a supreme exhibition of a skillful performance. A sigh of pure pleasure escaped Reuben; he was going to see his dream come true.

Henry now began to adjust driving goggles over his eyes and pull long leather gauntlets on his hands. He adjusted levers and pedals mysteriously, then climbed out to crank the motor. There was an ear-splitting roar and a series of sputtering coughs, and he ran back to adjust a lever under the steering wheel. The motor purred smoothly. With great care, he maneuvered himself into exactly the right position in the driver's seat. They all sat completely silent, watching his every move intently, almost reverently.

A sudden burst of smoke and scattered gravel, and they were out of the driveway and into the road. Reuben's stomach almost seemed to leap into his throat. For a moment his teeth chattered. He felt both fear and exhilaration at the same time.

"We're going better than fifteen an hour," shouted Gus over the roar of the motor. "Watch the trees, how they fly past!"

But Grandpa was not watching any trees. He did not even attempt an answer. He sat rigidly erect, staring straight ahead and holding to his hat with both hands. His lips were set in a firm, almost grim line. "Like he was fighting a battle," thought Reuben, stealing a quick look at Grandpa's face.

Reuben let go of the edge of the seat long enough to reach up and pull the ear flaps of

95

his cap down. It threatened to fly off his head at any moment as they flew over ruts and holes and rocks in the road. But there were surprisingly few hard bumps. Rubber tires and shock absorbers did make a difference in comfort.

Now they were whirling merrily out onto the river road north of town. Grandpa only turned for one quick look at the river, then resumed his rigid, eyes-front position, but Gus was looking around at the scenery and enjoying it.

When they came to a particularly fine lookout, up a small hill, Henry pulled up and stopped. Then he turned off the motor and climbed out to stretch. Grandpa was able to relax at last, and took out his watch. He spoke reluctantly, as if hating to admit it: "I can't believe it! Not twenty minutes since we left the Soldiers' Home—and so nice and easy. It's a nine-days' wonder!"

He and Gus looked out at the river, remembering the old days as loggers on this very part of the river. Their job had been to keep the logs moving, to prevent them from massing and tangling, so that they would flow steadily into the wide, still water above the saw mill. It was a dangerous and difficult job, requiring that they jump from log to log in the treacherous and swirling water, with their pike poles or peaveys in hands.

Grandpa located the scene of the "big jam" in '57, and Gus held up his crutch to point to a spot far out where he had once lost his footing. "But for Tim Mulvaney I would have drowned for sure—so they told me," he said. "There I was in the icy water, stunned-like, and a log bearing down from behind, swift and murderous. It was so close it woulda broke my neck in a few seconds if it hadn't been for Tim. He came leaping from log to log and held out his cant hook. I took hold and he pulled me out just in time!"

"Ah, yes," Grandpa said, "the logging days took their toll in lives. Erik, Mike Flynn,

Holger—my own son. And 'twas cruel, hard work, too. Plenty of men got rich through lumber, though not the likes of you and me. Still I don't really care about that. But when I recollect how the country looked then — as beautiful all over as it is in this one spot—then I wish we hadn't torn down the woods and made so much bald, useless land. But you know how it was, Gus. We were young and husky and poor—anxious for any kind of work that was to be had. We was only too glad then they wanted the trees cut down."

6

A Little Gasoline Is All It Takes

With Reuben at his heels, Henry was walking around the car, examining it carefully on each side. He pressed the tires hard with his fingers, explaining to Reuben what a dreaded thing a flat tire or a blow-out could be in motoring. He lifted the hinged metal sheet which he called the hood and studied the motor carefully. Reuben followed every move with fascinated interest. He tried to memorize as much as he could about the workings of an automobile. At the same time, he couldn't help listening to the conversation of the two old men.

Gus was talking now. "But think of the progress we have made since then—what we

100

have seen in just our time, Sven! Fifty years ago we had nothing in our pockets and had to depend on the strength of our backs alone in this raw, rough territory."

Grandpa was not in full agreement. "Life was good in those times, too," he said stubbornly. "I mind the joy I had in buying my land and clearing a piece and putting in a crop. Hard it was, sure, but it's something I never fergit, the satisfaction I had."

"But look at the progress since then," Gus went on, smiling. "Look at my nephew, Henry, now—how much more he's got than we did. Take the aut'mobile. . . ." He spoke the word slowly and importantly.

Grandpa smiled, but skeptically. "I'm not sure these rigs are real progress—not yet anyway. They're fine to ride in, sure. But our country lives mainly by agriculture, you know, and they can't take the place of horses there. Way I see it, we'll always be depending on horses mostly."

"Horses!" snorted Gus. "Time is coming— mark my words—when a horse will be little more than a curiosity. Even the crops will be harvested with gasoline-engine machines."

"No, now you go too far!" said Grandpa. "I don't believe that. Remember the team of mules we drove off that plantation near Atlanta, the ones the owners had run off and left and they was starving and thirsty when we found 'em? Remember them mules, Gus? They got to be one of the best mule teams in all Uncle Billy's army! You remember, don't you, Gus?"

Grandpa seemed to be trying to steer the conversation back to the war years, bringing up experiences they had shared. There were so few who wanted to hear about these now. This was the reason he had always found the companionship of Gus so good; they had always been able to talk about their soldiering days without either of them becoming tired or wanting to change the subject.

102

But today Gus seemed interested only in the present. He was proud of his nephew for having an automobile, one of the finest in the whole town of Stillwater. It had given him an importance that he found altogether new and exciting. His mind was not really on his friend's wartime recollections as they sat gazing down at the winding river. The weekly ride was the biggest thing in his life now.

"Yah, I remember," he said, stroking the red upholstery almost lovingly. "But I want you should enjoy this ride, Sven. Think what little work there is with a machine like this! No hitching or unhitching, no feeding or watering, and no stable to clean! A little gasoline is all it takes, and you don't even have to get out of the car to get it. You stop at a gas station and sit in the car like a gentleman while the gasoline is poured in."

"Very nice," admitted Grandpa. "But what I'd like best is not having any worry about horses' ailments like sore feet or glanders or heaves. You don't have to call the horse doctor for a ottymobile—that's something!"

He laughed heartily at his own joke and took out his watch. "But now we ought to be getting back, I think. It's almost a quarter to four."

Henry obligingly prepared to leave. He set the lever carefully and went forward to crank. Reuben watched every move, intent on memorizing the steps required to start a motor. But this time when the crank was turned, nothing happened. There was a slight sputter, but the answering roar did not come. Over and over he repeated the process, but each time the sputter grew more faint.

"Funny," he said, looking puzzled and worried. "She won't start."

Gus looked around. "Mebbe it's just too big a load. I bet that's the trouble, Henry. You never had two in the back seat before. Heavy people, too."

Reuben jumped out quickly, eager to be of

help, but Henry spoke irritably. "You don't know nothing about it, Uncle Gus. Number of passengers in a car has nothing to do with how it starts. Sounds more like she's out of gas."

He picked up a small stick and measured the amount of gasoline in the tank attached to the side of the car. "Yes, sir—that's it!" he said triumphantly after a moment. "She's almost dry, and I'm parked on a slope so what there is has run into one end of the tank."

It appeared to be a great relief to Henry to find this reasonable excuse for the motor failure. "Just one thing to do, I guess," he said. "Get out the little red can and ride shanks' mare to the gas station we passed about a mile back."

Gus sat staring at the river in humiliated silence. Grandpa's expression was one of gloomy scorn, as he took out his watch and looked at it again.

"Progress, you were sayin', Gus!" He snorted suddenly in derision. "This is progress? Better

than horses, eh? Well, one thing I know—you don't have to put gasoline in a horse to make him run. He runs best on an empty stomach."

Reuben was suddenly uneasy. One mile back — that meant two to be walked. It was already almost four o'clock. He could not help remembering that he had been entrusted with the responsibility of seeing that they got started home on time. Never mind that it had been Grandpa's decision to take the automobile ride. It was he who had said confidently, "Don't worry, nothing will go wrong." How would he ever be able to explain to Papa?

Reuben began to run after Henry. "I'm coming with you," he panted. "Maybe we can walk faster if there are the two of us."

They walked very fast and talked hardly at all. Henry answered Reuben's questions shortly, so after a while Reuben, too, became silent and trotted along without a word.

When they had returned, and the gasoline was poured into the tank, there were a few moments of tense silence as the crank-up process began again. But this time the motor started. Again Henry adjusted everything, including goggles and gloves, and they were off.

Grandpa sat more rigid with distrust now than before. He looked neither to the right nor the left, though Gus tried now and then to interest him in the scenery. It was plain that he wanted the ride to be over as quickly as possible, and nothing more.

Henry drove fast and they were back at the Soldiers' Home by five o'clock. Grandpa climbed out hastily and turned to Henry, speaking politely. "Thanks for the ride," he said. "It was—a real experience; one I won't likely fergit."

He shook hands with Gus and told him that he would come to visit again "maybe some time in the summer." But he made it clear that he preferred that visit to be in the rocking chairs on the veranda rather than in an automobile.

With Reuben's help the stamping, restive horses were untied. Grandpa scrambled up in the wagon with a good push from behind; Reuben quickly followed, and they were on their way home.

7

The Runaway

The horses were showing their hunger; they raced along at furious speed. "At this rate we'll make it home by seven," said Grandpa. "That won't be so late, after all. The way I see it, your Pa was mostly worried that we'd be on the road after dark, but, like as not, we'll make it by sundown."

However, he was no longer in a mood for quiet recollections. He sputtered angrily now and then about fine-looking motorcars that became helpless and immovable for lack of gasoline. How could you trust that kind of contraption? Misfortune could come to a country if it depended on such unreliable machinery, he pointed out sagely.

Reuben thought it rather unfair to blame the automobile for what was obviously Henry's carelessness in failing to have the gas tank filled. But he sat quiet as the old man sputtered on; it seemed to relieve Grandpa's nerves to express his irritation with the automobile.

In spite of the old man's apparent unconcern about their late arrival home, Reuben was worried. He felt chiefly to blame, even though Grandpa kept saying magnanimously that he "would do the explainin'." He, Reuben, was the one who had been especially entrusted with the safety and success of the trip, and Papa would consider the late arrival an accident hazard such as those he was constantly warning against. "Close all gates; keep fences tight; know how to handle horses; don't be on the road late. . . ." Reuben had heard such admonitions as long as he could remember. They'd had their effect, too, on Will and Johnny, who were serious and careful about

111

everything they did, while he was always being reprimanded.

But maybe luck would be on their side. If Papa and the boys were working late—especially if they were in the cornfield beyond the woodland—they would not be there to see the exact time he and Grandpa arrived. Mama would not likely give them away; she would just forget to look at the clock. And Reuben himself would see carefully to the rubdown and feeding of the team.

Grandpa pulled on the reins hard and talked soothingly to the horses. "Whoa, there —slow down now! You'll be home in your own stalls soon. Give over, now!" He looked worried as his hands tightened their hold and his legs braced themselves against the dashboard. "Seems I can hardly hold 'em in," he said. "It's bad to be on the road this time of day with hungry horses. They get kinda wild. Still they're bound to tire soon."

An automobile approached suddenly from

behind, sounding its horn loudly. It was a horrid, frightening sound—something halfway between a dog's bark and the honking of a goose. Grandpa all but jumped out of the wagon seat, but he managed to hug the right side of the road and to pull the horses to a walk as the motorcar approached, raising a cloud of dust.

But at the moment of passing, the grinning driver could not resist showing off a bit. He gave another blast of the horn. "EEE—AWK!" barked the whirring monster machine, and the horses threw up their heads in terror and plunged into a wild gallop.

Grandpa pulled frantically on the reins, but it was quite useless. With fright added to their impatience, the horses were simply too strong for him.

"Whoa! Whoa!" roared Grandpa, alternately with words like "There, Ned — good boy! Stop now, Fanny!" But the frightened team plunged on, and the light wagon rattled along like an eggshell about to break in pieces at any moment.

Grandpa held on tightly, his gnarled hands laced through the stiff rawhide of the reins. Reuben, clinging to the edge of his seat in fright, managed a glance at Grandpa's face. It seemed frozen in fear. How long would those arms hold out? The horses showed no signs of tiring. Grandpa was an old man—how many times had he not heard that from everyone? He had been unwilling to believe what this meant before. But now it showed; Grandpa was simply not equal to this desperate situation.

Suddenly, almost without being conscious of what he was doing, Reuben slid off the seat and onto his knees on the floor of the wagon. He planted himself between Grandpa's legs and reached up to put his hands on the reins in front of Grandpa's straining hands. He began to pull with all his strength. He would make the horses feel that! Two pairs of hands

should be able to hold them on the road, at least for a while until they got tired.

Behind him, Grandpa panted gratefully. "That's right, boy! Help me hold 'em in. Seems like I ain't got no strength no more. My arms is beginnin' to give out."

"Just hang on and don't fall out!" Reuben shouted back encouragingly. "We'll pull them in together!"

His lips were set in a firm line and he stared straight ahead. Bits of gritty foam and sweat from the horses flew into his eyes and mouth; his nostrils were dry and dust-clogged. But he held on desperately, for it was clear that their only hope lay in riding out the runaway. If they could keep the horses on the road, prevent them from plunging into the ditch, they might avert disaster. Maddened horses were likely to do crazy things; that was why runaways all too often meant broken bones or even more serious injuries. No one knew this better than Reuben. But still, horses were

116

horses—they had only so much strength. They simply would have to tire after a while. "They can't keep it up forever," he said to himself grimly.

A few more minutes of desperate strain, and he gasped out happily, "They're slowing down! They're getting tired! We've won, Grandpa!"

As suddenly as it began, the runaway was over. Feeling no relaxation of the pull on the reins, the horses finally gave up and slowed to a trot. The trot became a walk as the frightened beasts, now utterly spent, seemed to be trying to regain their equanimity. They snorted and blew and neighed in short bursts of noise, as if to reassure each other that the danger from the monster machine was past. Slowly Reuben relaxed his hold on the reins and climbed back into his place on the seat. He let out a long, gusty sigh of relief as he wiped his gritty face all over with a handkerchief. His voice, when he was able to talk, sounded

117

small and weak. "They're all right now; I guess they're about as tired as we are. I bet they'll walk the rest of the way."

Grandpa's face looked gray, both with dust and fright. His eyes were bloodshot and watery. When he finally spoke, his voice quavered pitifully.

"Boy, that were a close call!" He passed a trembling hand across his eyes. "I thought sure we was done for. Expected any minute we'd be tipped in the ditch with the wagon over us. It woulda served me right for takin' that fool ride. Knowin' the horses, I had no business . . . my fault entirely. . . ." His lips moved like those of a child about to cry, and he was unable to go on.

It was embarrassing to Reuben to see Grandpa so weak, even close to tears, although he did not feel particularly strong himself at that moment. To relieve feelings, he exploded crossly, "Well, gee whiz! If you ask me, neither horses nor automobiles are exactly perfect.

118

Seems like they both can give you plenty of trouble. A person's own legs — what Henry called 'shanks' mare' — seems about the only safe way to travel."

He had said exactly the right thing to help Grandpa regain his calm and to set him reminiscing about the old days.

"Well, now, I sure have to agree with you there. And you know, that's all we had there at first. Take the reins a minute. I need a bit of a smoke bad.

"Why, when I'd taken my claim, I had neither horse nor mule to work it with. I cut down trees and grubbed out stumps by the strength of my own back. Sometimes your Grandma would help, of course. The two of us would hitch ourselves to a rope, just like a team, and then heave and pull with all our might. You'd be surprised how strong the two of us was together!

"And then, of course, there was John, our son. What a help that boy were! But, well—

119

never mind that now. Seems though, some-times you remind me of him a good deal. He woulda done just what you did in the runaway back there, I b'lieve. Oh, he was brave, and smart, too, that boy. . . ."

Reuben cleared his throat noisily. He swung one leg over the edge of the wagon in the carefree manner of young men drivers. The bond between him and Grandpa was drawn closer than ever by the runaway. He saw clearly that though neither of them was very strong by himself alone, together they could be almost unbeatable.

Grandpa's pipe glowed brightly and he puffed on it placidly. "Let me tell you 'bout a bit of walkin' I did," he began. "Came a day that first year on our own claim when I needed a grindstone bad. I *had* to have one, you might say. The axe and the hoe and the scythe all needed sharpenin', you know. I tried to borry a horse or even a pair of mules or an ox from someone so's I could drive to Marine and get me a grindstone. That was our closest town then.

"But everyone was busy with their own work and using their animals themselves full time, so they put me off. They told me I'd have to wait until they could spare something to drive with. Well, sir, I weren't of a mind to wait, with my work waitin' to be done, and all my tools dull and useless. So one mornin' I got up early, did my chores, and then walked down to Marine. I bought my grindstone, put it on my back, took a drink of water, and started for home again. It were hot that day, too, but I made it home in time for the evenin' chores."

"Almost fourteen miles! And carrying a heavy stone all the way back!" Reuben whistled softly. "That must have been even harder than a day on the march with Sherman."

"It were," said Grandpa judiciously. "I warn't in trainin' like when we marched close to fifteen miles a day regular. But even the

121

long walk, carryin' the heavy stone and all—that warn't thought so much of in them days. Everyone worked hard one way or 'nother. If a thing had to be done, you did it without too much talk or fuss about it. It was the idee we lived by, you know; we wouldn't have got our farms started without it. Now, with the new machinery comin' on so fast—ridin' plows, harrows, seeders, and that wonderful new harvestin' machine and all—such olden-time work as we did may seem a bit unbelievable. But we didn't think it remarkable then. We just took it for our share of work and did it."

Grandpa paused, looking off at the dying sunset. Reuben sat quiet beside him, thinking. It *was* remarkable all the same, he reflected. People ought to know how hard men like Grandpa had worked in those early days. Likely some people never knew, or cared either, how the farms got started.

"I guess we should remember such things more," was all he said.

The team plodded along very slowly, and Grandpa made no effort to hurry them, even though dusk was beginning to fall. He had been watching Ned closely for some minutes and now he leaned forward suddenly, peering at the right front foot of the big horse.

"Blast that jessie rig anyway!" he said finally in disgust. "Ned's cast a shoe. Musta happened in the runaway, but I didn't notice it until just now. Could mean real trouble; he's walkin' more lame every step."

"What'll we do?" asked Reuben, realizing with dismay that they were only halfway home.

"Well, I s'pose we could go on this way, slow and careful, and maybe no harm would be done. But since we go by there, I think we'd best stop at the blacksmith's in Marine and have him put on a new shoe. It'll save your Pa a trip, too; this time of year he needs all his horses, and we'd better not risk a sore foot."

Grandpa spoke briskly, again a man of action and authority. "If the smith still has a fire in his forge, the shoein' won't take too long. Olson works pretty fast." He spoke soothingly to Ned, letting him pick his way along the road slowly.

It was almost dark as they rounded Morgan's Hill and entered the main street of the tiny, quiet village of Marine. They passed the general store, now closed. Old Growler, the watchdog, noted for his fierce bark, was chained up on the porch. Though he was partly deaf, he still managed to keep prowlers away from the store premises effectively. He set up loud barking and deep-throated growling whenever a strange foot came up the porch steps. A tiny light showed at the back, indicating where the telephone company's Central girl was on duty at the new switchboard. Opposite the store was the bank, the most imposing structure in the village, and halfway down the same street there was a church and a small boardinghouse hotel. The street was deserted, and the houses seemed closed up for the night.

At the very end of the street was the blacksmith shop, and the smithy doors stood open. They could see the glow from the forge inside.

"Good," said Grandpa. "Smith Olson is likely in the house, eatin' his supper. Go knock on the door there and tell him our trouble."

The blacksmith, a huge swarthy man with dark, hairy arms and a kind and gentle face, stood up immediately at Reuben's story. Picking up a small lantern from a table, he hurried outside, pulling on a jacket.

"Oh, it's you, Sven! A runaway, eh? Bad! And for a man your age too. . . . But I shoe your horse good—and quick. No worry." He went into the shop and began to pump up the dying coals with a bellows. "Fire hot soon. We fix Ned good as new."

The fire burned up brightly and the smith puttered around getting out tools and nails as Grandpa and Reuben got Ned out of harness.

They led him into the shop and the blacksmith lifted his foot to examine it. Ned stood completely still.

"He acts as if you're a doctor," said Reuben. Ned gave a short whinny, and they all laughed. He seemed to be actually trying to give symptoms.

"And so I am," said the smith proudly. He took a knife and began to trim the hoof. Next he used a long file to smooth it carefully all over. "I'm a foot doctor for horses, you might say. I never put on shoe until I first fix foot nice and smooth so new shoe fits right. Walking on overgrown hoofs and bad fitting shoes can make all kinds of trouble for horse. And where is farmer if his horse don't walk good?"

"But we aren't always going to have to depend on horses, you know," said Reuben. "A man told us today the time is coming soon when they'll be driving entirely with automobiles. They'll even be doing all kinds of farming with gasoline engines some day—pretty soon too. Horse-drawn machinery will be as old-fashioned as ox-carts are now."

The smith, with Ned's foot between his legs, smiled indulgently. He lifted the glowing horseshoe from the forge and shaped it with a few quick strokes of the hammer, then began fitting it to the hoof with care, hammering in the nails with swift, powerful strokes.

"Sure," he said, puffing slightly. "Like big flying machines some day take place of trains and ships! You believe such stories, too, liddle boy?" He glanced over at Grandpa, giving a broad wink. Reuben could see that the weight of opinion was against him, but he held his ground.

"I've heard about them," he said boldly. "And I think the time is coming some day when airships will be used for long trips — maybe even to fly across the ocean!"

The smith, feeling that this remark was too silly to deserve comment, remained silent, absorbed with his job of shoeing Ned.

8

The Two Prove Unbeatable

Grandpa had been puttering outside with the wagon as the blacksmith finished his work. The runaway had loosened more than Ned's shoe, and the old man had been busy with the wrench, tightening bolts and screws. Finally he lighted the buggy lamps, one on each side of the wagon. By now it was dark; the blacksmith was working in a little pool of lantern light inside the shop.

At last the shoeing was completed and Ned was put back in harness. Grandpa paid Smith Olson, politely declining his offer to come in for a bite of supper, because of the lateness of the hour.

They exchanged farewells and the blacksmith took his lantern and went back into the house. Reuben had begun to help Grandpa up into the seat when two men, who had been standing in the shadows across the street, came swiftly and directly toward them. Reuben thought at first they must be wanting a ride, but as they came within range of the buggy lights, he saw that they had bandanna handkerchiefs tied over the lower part of their faces. Above these, their eyes seemed to glow like dark coals.

The taller of the two men held out his arm in a gesture that seemed almost natural and friendly until something in his hand gleamed dully in the light of the buggy lamp. Though he had never seen one before, Reuben knew what it was. He had seen pictures of revolvers, and the boys at school often talked about them.

The truth seemed to come to Grandpa at the same moment. He bent close to Reuben and whispered one word: "Robbers!"

Now the taller of the two men spoke, very

131

softly, but menacingly. "Get away from that wagon," he said, moving toward them. "Just leave your team tied up there. We'll be needing it soon. You and the boy get back into the shop." He moved his hand back and forth in a slight gesture that covered them both with the ugly little weapon. "Get going, Gramp!" He roughly pushed the old man toward the smithy door with his free hand. The other man was firmly pushing Reuben forward at the same time.

Grandpa's face showed starkly white in the dim glow of the lamps. His short legs teetered slightly as he reached up stiffly with his arms to show that he had no weapon and wanted no trouble.

"That's right," the smaller man said coaxingly. "We don't want any trouble, you know. Do just like we say and no one is going to get hurt at all."

He spoke almost gently, as if by nature he were really a reasonable, kindly soul and

wanted to show that he did not belong in this job and company at all.

The experience was beginning to have an unreal quality both to Reuben and to Grandpa. They moved dazedly. This was the sort of thing one read about in the newspapers, but always with the feeling that it could never happen to ordinary folks. Now Reuben realized, with a tightening throat, it *was* happening—and it was happening to them!

"Why should anyone try to rob Grandpa?" Reuben wondered. Of course, they couldn't know that after the shoeing of Ned, he had less than a dollar left in his pocketbook. "It's some kind of mistake, that's all," he thought. When the robbers discovered their mistake, no doubt the nightmare would be over. He and Grandpa would be turned loose and be free to go.

But there were no hopeful signs of this happening now. At the door of the smithy, Reuben turned and cast a quick, despairing glance up the deserted street. Was there no one at all around to come to their help? Surely someone would be passing by, even on this quiet edge of the little town!

But all was darkness and silence except for the plaintive bellowing of a calf in a pasture close by, and a chorus of loudly singing frogs in the roadside ditches. Despite these dear, homely sounds, the fragrant spring evening seemed filled with nameless terror.

Now Reuben was gripped by a chilly fear that maybe the men were going to hurt Grandpa—maybe even shoot him—for some senseless reason. He felt no great worry for himself; after all, who would bother to do anything to a boy? It was the old soldier who was in some real danger. Perhaps he was regarded as a threat to whatever evil scheme the men had in mind.

Reuben made up his mind for a desperate try. Just inside the doorway, he ducked suddenly and bolted. But long legs overtook him and an iron hand caught him and held him in a vise-like grip that left him limp.

He managed to bluster feebly, "You'd better not try anything—"

"Get in there," snarled the tall man, jerking him like a rag doll. "Don't *you* be trying any monkeyshines, or you'll wish you hadn't!"

Grandpa spoke softly out of the darkness. "Do what they say, boy." For the benefit of the men, he added apologetically, "He didn't mean nothin' — pay him no mind. We'll give you no trouble. Just don't hurt the boy."

Suddenly Reuben was tripped and thrown to the floor. Lengths of twine were whipped around his ankles and tightly knotted. His legs had swiftly been made completely immovable. Now his wrists were being tied, and so tightly that he cried out in pain. It was a relief to find his voice again, and he began to yell: "Help! Help! Hey! Robbers!"

But a hand smelling of dirt and tobacco closed over his mouth. Then a handkerchief was stuffed in it and another tied tightly over it, making a complete and effective gag. Again and again, Reuben tried to cry out, to make some kind of sound, but only a dull, throaty gurgle came out. His mouth tasted snuff and dirt worse than before.

His eyes were becoming used to the darkness now. In the dim glow of the forge he could see that Grandpa also lay on the smithy floor, quite close to the forge where the blacksmith had recently been working over Ned's foot. The other man was busy tying him up, and a gag had already been put over his mouth.

Their job with the prisoners done, the two men stood together talking earnestly and quietly. Reuben strained his ears and caught snatches of conversation here and there.

". . . tools? . . . combination . . . in my pocket . . . easy job. . . ." He could tell that it was the shorter man speaking; his high voice was almost wheedling.

The other voice came gruffly, but more

137

softly so that the words were harder to hear. He made out nothing except the words 'slip-up' and 'no chances' but judging by the tone, it was clear that he was admonishing the other and possibly accusing him of something.

"Scandia Center . . . your slip-up, I'd say!" The high voice rose accusingly in argument. "I hate shooting!"

". . . in my way . . . had to. Quiet! Look sharp now!"

They stood together at the door. A lumber wagon rumbled by slowly, and they ducked quickly inside. Reuben could see them quite clearly. He strained his ears to catch their words and was rewarded by hearing a summing up of their plan. Again it was the high voice speaking. "No one notices team here . . . run back, unhitch . . . midnight Flyer. . . ."

Reuben heard the sudden quick shuffle of feet as they went outside, then the double doors were softly closed and footsteps retreated rapidly.

Reuben lay twisting his hands in the dark silence. The strong bonds held firm and the slight moves he was able to make only lacerated his wrists. Tools—combination—the Scandia job! Why, these were the men who had robbed the Scandia Center bank two weeks ago! One of them, most likely the big, mean-talking one, was believed to have been originally with the James-Younger gang that had operated in Minnesota some years before. Now the two of them were planning to rob the Marine bank—were on their way to do it right now! Suddenly it was perfectly clear.

This was the way they had done the Scandia Center job, according to the constable's story the day after, when he'd stopped at home to talk to Papa: A strange man had come into the bank a few days before the robbery, apparently to talk about a western land deal he was promoting. He was a small man, with an ingratiating voice, who had so impressed the cashier and his assistant that they had almost

139

Reuben's hands clawed angrily at the dirt floor of the smithy. The sharp twine cut his hands at every move. He bit furiously at the dirty bandanna but succeeded only in getting it further into his mouth. Tears of rage came into his eyes. These were mean, dangerous men who would stop at nothing. And he and Grandpa were completely helpless!

There was a Flyer train through Stillwater just before midnight; if they caught it they would have all night in which to make their getaway. Their planning was perfect, Reuben reflected angrily.

"They'll be using our team to help them pull off this crime. And if anyone should happen to get in their way, anything may happen!"

He kept on writhing and twisting and making gurgling sounds in his throat. His wrists and ankles were beginning to ache from trying to loosen the bonds, but the twine held firmly. He hoped they had not tied up Grandpa so terribly tight; he had enough trouble with his legs already. He raised his head to look at Grandpa, for now his eyes were becoming used to the darkness. It was a relief at least to know that they had not hurt the old man. He strained his eyes and stared. Grandpa was lying closer to the forge now than a few minutes ago. Could he possibly have moved?

Yes, by the dim glow of the coals, Reuben saw that Grandpa was definitely moving himself forward, in spite of tightly bound hands and feet. He was twisting and writhing his solid frame in a way Reuben would not have believed possible, stiff as he was with rheumatism, and tied up besides. What could be in his mind? It would be impossible to get to the door, and impossible to open it, even if he should manage to get that far.

When he reached the forge, Grandpa lay still for a few moments as if utterly spent with his exertions. Then suddenly, with a great effort, he rolled over on his side. It was obvious that he had some sort of plan in mind.

142

Reuben watched in fascination. He saw Grandpa's two hands, still bound together, grasp and pick up something from the floor. It was the long file the blacksmith had used on Ned's hoof. Grandpa used it now as a sort of cane to raise himself up to a kneeling position. Next he began struggling to get to his feet, but his stiff, tightly bound old legs could not quite manage this. So, still kneeling, with his tied-up hands grasping the file, he pushed it into the glowing coals of the forge.

He was up to something, though he could not communicate it to Reuben. "Good, brave Grandpa!" thought Reuben, with loving admiration. "I might have known he'd think of something."

Reuben now began a determined forward writhing on the floor himself. He was surprised to find that it was possible to move forward quite fast this way. He edged toward Grandpa and the forge by using his shoulders and legs in a twisting, snake-like motion. He reached

Grandpa's side. Grandpa nodded his head vigorously and approvingly. Obviously, this was what he wanted him to do. By steadying himself against Grandpa's solid bulk, Reuben managed to get to his feet. Again he was rewarded by an approving nod.

With his tightly tied hands, Grandpa was reaching again toward the forge. He took hold of the file handle even though the other end was glowing dull red from the heat of the fire. Grandpa pointed it at Reuben's wrists and looked hard at him. His eyes above the gag were earnest and pleading; it was as if he were trying to tell Reuben something.

Reuben began to get the idea. "He's telling me that he means to burn the twine off and free my hands!" He edged closer to Grandpa and immediately held out his hands.

Grandpa carefully poked the file at the cords in the small space where Reuben was able to hold his hands apart slightly. Then he began pushing the file back and forth in a saw-

144

ing motion. Now and then the hot iron touched wrists or hands, and Reuben winced with pain. But he stiffened resolutely, telling himself that it would soon be over, and a few burns would not matter.

The cords began to smoke. In a few moments they were burned through enough so that he was able to break them with a strong twist of his hands. As he did so, he felt the smarting of raw flesh. He untied his own gag swiftly and then the one on Grandpa. They both wiped their mouths, trying to rid themselves of the taste of dirty cloth.

"Must be the Scandia Center bank robbers!" Reuben gasped.

"Figgers," said Grandpa shortly. "Same voices I heard that day I was in town—the ones what hid when I turned to look. I'm certain of it."

While Reuben was freeing his legs, Grandpa began talking rapidly and decisively like a battle commander before an attack. "No time

to set me free. Just do what I say *exactly*.
'Member how I tightened the rear wheels
while the smith worked on Ned? The wrench
—it's under the back seat. Get it and loosen
the nuts on the two right wheels until they
come off. Then just barely stick them on again
—one turn with your hand will do it. Got that?"
Reuben nodded, though he was puzzled.

"No time for explaining. Just do what I say.
It'll be as much as we dare to risk. They'll be
back any time, and you mustn't be seen. Lay
down in the bushes if you see 'em comin' afore
you're done. If you have time, come in and lay
down like you was tied up; they may look in
here, you know. When they drive off, we'll call
the constable and sheriff both. Hurry now!
Close the doors after you so they don't get
suspicious. And don't let 'em see you!"

Reuben did not wait to hear more. Grandpa
must have some sort of plan in mind, though
he could not tell Reuben what it was.

No use thinking about the ugly possibility

of what might happen if the robbers came back into the smithy and found Grandpa there alone. They'd know then that he, Reuben, was up to something—maybe out to give an alarm. Grandpa might pay with his life for daring to attempt to outwit them. But he wouldn't think about that. He must follow orders, trusting to Grandpa's judgment.

The doors, loosely held together with a wooden bolt, yielded to the hard lunge of his body, and he found himself outside. He quickly closed the doors, placing the bolt in place again. It was the work of a few minutes to loosen the nuts on the two wagon wheels, and then, as Grandpa had instructed, he just barely stuck them back on again.

As he brushed past Ned, the horse gave a short whinny as if asking what this was all about. Reuben patted him hastily on the flank and whispered, "Don't worry, Ned boy! We'll fix 'em. They won't have you long!"

He glanced up the dark street. At the far

148

end was the bank, and directly across from it the general store with the telephone office in back. They had seen its light still on as they drove past a short while ago. If he could make it there and give the alarm to Central before the men got back! Was it too wild an idea? At any moment now they would come running down the street. They would grab the team and make their getaway. Grandpa had warned him that he mustn't be seen, and he could well imagine the consequences to both of them if he were. He crouched low beside a clump of bushes, wavering between fear and courageous daring.

If he could keep to the shadows of hedges and bushes all the way up the street. . . . He would need only to dash out in the open once, to get across the street to the store and Central office. The men's backs would be toward him as they ran for the smithy. It was a risk worth taking, if only to keep the rascals from trying anything with Grandpa.

He began to run, keeping to the shadows on the right side of the street. On the left was a deep ditch filled with water and there was little shrubbery for protection. Here and there on this side too, there were shallow depressions filled with muddy water, making the running difficult. But he managed to stay hidden behind trees and shrubbery, leaping along quietly from one pool of shade to another.

Suddenly in the light of the lamppost directly in front of the bank, he saw the side door of the bank open cautiously. A man's figure was briefly silhouetted in the doorway. Then the door was thrown open and the two men came running toward him, heads down, with long, loping strides.

Reuben dropped to his knees in the shallow ditch, then flat on his stomach. There seemed to be more frogs and mud than water, and the harsh croaking chorus of the frogs covered any noise he might have made. A big elm overhead threw its shadow over him as he lay shivering in the muck. He was close enough to the bank and the store now so the street light illuminated everything faintly. The robbers' feet trotted by so close that he could have reached out his hand and tripped them.

When they had passed, he jumped up noiselessly and darted across the street. The men were almost to the smithy now. But he was in front of the store—almost at the telephone office! He had time to wonder briefly what people had done in such emergencies before they had telephones. It had been only a little more than a year that they'd had the Central office in Marine, but it made everyone sleep more securely to know that the Central girl slept there at night, so she could take care of emergency calls. She was seldom bothered after nine o'clock, but now....Well, she would be making some important calls in a couple of minutes!

Reuben turned to look down the street. He had to be sure they hadn't gone into the

151

smithy again. They must be down there by now. What was taking them so long? The lights on the wagon were still glowing softly, and there was not the slightest movement to indicate that the men were getting ready to drive off. What would happen if they went in and found Grandpa alone?

He must do something to frighten them away—to scare them into driving off quickly. But how? Old Growly—that was it! Already he could hear the ominous deep-throated growls from the store doorway. He must get him to bark. He ran up the steps and across the wooden porch, grabbed the dog's chain and jerked it hard. The huge bulldog leaped up and began to bark. Reuben stepped back quickly and kept carefully out of reach of the animal. He stood listening a moment as the sound reverberated down the street, and suddenly he saw that there was activity around the wagon. The robbers were not about to linger around the smithy a moment longer now. They were making their getaway fast.

Reuben ran around to the back of the store and pounded hard on the telephone office door. The Central girl came quickly and opened the door to him. He had only to say "Bank robbery!" and she was at the switchboard plugging in calls. As she went about her business efficiently, he gave her the main facts. Short staccato rings were being buzzed to constable and sheriff at the same time.

She had just got the constable on the line when they heard the swift crunch of wheels and pound of hooves outside on the road. Reuben was sure he recognized the familiar gallop of Ned and Fanny.

The robbers were on their way then. They were taking the Stillwater road as they had planned, to catch the midnight Flyer. There was nothing more for him to do now. He had gone against Grandpa's orders, and he'd have to explain that somehow. But he still felt that the risk of being seen by the men had been

worth taking in order to give the alarm as quickly as possible, just in case they had gone back into the blacksmith shop to try something mean with Grandpa. He was sure when he explained this, Grandpa would understand.

Suddenly he was very tired and cold. His clothes were wet and muddy, and he was becoming increasingly aware of sharp, throbbing pain in his hands and wrists. He wanted only to get back to the blacksmith shop, to make sure that Grandpa was all right.

Having told Central all he could, he turned and ran out of the door. She was still busy at the switchboard, giving information in a clear, concise voice.

Reuben's feet felt strangely light and his head seemed to float weightlessly on his neck as he ran down the silent street. He was suddenly aware of intense pain in his hands and wrists. He thought they must be burned much worse than he had felt at the time Grandpa had used the hot file. But of course, then he had been so excited just to get loose, he hadn't thought about anything else. Now the danger was past and he was beginning to feel the pain.

But there was still Grandpa. Reuben pushed open the smithy doors fearfully, wondering what he would find. He saw that Grandpa still lay where he had left him, but he lay ominously still.

As Reuben bent over him, the old eyes opened and looked up anxiously into his face. But even in the dim glow of the dying coals Reuben could detect a faint reassuring smile. Suddenly he felt no pain or floaty feeling at all—only a blessed sense of relief.

"Don't look so scared, boy," said Grandpa. "I'm not hurt. Pay me no mind if I look kinda seedy. It's only that I'm feelin' a mite tired. And I got worried when you didn't come back in soon as I heard 'em drive off. You all right? You manage to do what I told you with the wheels?"

Reuben was helping him to sit up. "Sure,"

he said, wincing with pain at the movement necessary in taking out his jackknife. He began cutting the twine from Grandpa's hands and feet, though the pain in his wrists was making him light-headed again. He pretended clumsiness. "Knife's awful dull—won't cut right," he mumbled. "Did the robbers come in here afterwards at all?"

"I heard 'em opening the door," said Grandpa. "I was groanin' and gruntin' something turrible, tryin' to make enough noise for two, you know, so they wouldn't look in. But they would have, oh yes, only then a dog started barkin' up the street—oh, such a racket he set up! Must have been old Growler, and he did scare them good! They just turned and ran for the wagon and next thing I heard 'em scramblin' into the wagon and whippin' up the horses. Way they drove off, I just wonder how long them wheels stayed on. But now, if my legs will hold me, we got to get the alarm out, and then do somethin' about those burns."

"I've already given the alarm. I had time, and it looked like a good chance so I ran to the Central office and she called—"

"You have?" Grandpa peered at him closely. He had noted the tremor in Reuben's voice and now he saw the raw, bleeding wrists and hands. It was apparent that they were hurting too much for Reuben to be able to talk further.

Reuben began to shiver again, for now the throbbing pains shot up the whole length of his arms, and these seemed to be feeling strangely big and puffy. He grimaced suddenly in his efforts to keep from crying.

Grandpa took charge swiftly. "All right then. We won't bother to talk now. We'll just go in Olson's house and call the doctor. But don't worry; it won't be too bad. And you've been such a brave boy up to now, it won't matter if you cry a little. It might even ease the hurt a bit."

9

The Constable Comes To Dinner

All the rest was a blur in Reuben's memory.
He had no clear recollection of anything that
took place after they got into Olson's kitchen.
The last thing he remembered, he was lying
on the sofa there and the pain was burning
fiercely. Then he saw the doctor take a kind
of big needle out of his bag. He stabbed it into
Reuben's arm. Suddenly the pain yielded to
a wonderful drowsiness that blotted out everything.

Now he was lying in his own bed at home.
He could tell that it was late in the morning
by the brightness of the sun streaming in the
window. For a few minutes he lay still in complete contentment. He remembered nothing

160

of the previous night's happenings until he looked at his hands lying in their big bandages on the quilt. Then suddenly everything began to come back. A few things were hazy and vague, fitting together imperfectly. Some of the wonderful blotting-out feeling that had stopped the pain last night still seemed to be left, making him feel drowsy and relaxed. He lay unmoving, looking up at the ceiling and feeling no particular desire to get up.

After a while he heard a man's voice coming up from the dining room below. He seemed to be talking almost continuously. The family must be at dinner. The voice was not Papa's or one that he recognized. He lay listening almost without interest. Then something in the way the r's were rolled struck him as familiar. Now who was it who talked that way — different from the familiar Scandinavian accents in their community?

Reuben sat up suddenly, wide awake. Of course! It was Mr. Campbell, the Marine village constable who had been there two weeks ago, that day after the Scandia Center bank robbery. Reuben had been fascinated with his way of talking—the "Scotch brogue" Mama had called it. He had it from being born in the "old country," which in his case was Scotland, just as their Scandinavian neighbors had their accents from their own "old countries," if they had not been long in America.

So now Mr. Campbell was here in their home, evidently having dinner with the family. Reuben was suddenly excited. It could mean only one thing; he must be here about the bank robbery. In one bound, Reuben was out of bed and crouching down at the heat register on the floor to listen.

"That business with the wheels," the constable was saying. "That was r-right clever of you, old fella. How in the wor-rld did you happen to think of it?"

Reuben heard Grandpa give a short, pleased chuckle. "Well, layin' there on the floor, trussed up like a hog and just as helpless, I said to meself: This is like nothin' I ever experienced in all my life — no sir, not even in the war!

"But then it come to me. I said to meself: now mebbe 'tis, if I kin just put my mind to figgerin' on it without worryin' so much. I minded how once when we was bummin' for food in Sherman's army, we come on some Reb gun carriages hidden away in a little clump of trees on a fine big plantation. We sent word to Captain, askin' what we should do 'bout them guns. He give orders to unscrew the nuts on the wheels just that same way. We hadn't much time, bein' on the march, you know, but this mischief stopped 'em so they never got started if they was aimin' to use them guns. We found out it was a guerrilla outfit hidin' in the big house that had hid the guns; they'd planned to attack our rear guard and cut 'em off. That would have decoyed part of the marchin' column back and killed some of our men and. . . ."

Grandpa stopped a moment, pausing for breath. He went on strongly: "By then the Rebs mighta got re-enforcements and coulda made a right smart amount of trouble for us. They coulda cut up the rear units bad.

"But when we went back there next day— dern, if we didn't find ever' one of those gun carriages broke down, with wheels off! Happened just the way Captain figgered, and it were just enough to confound and delay the enemy so they had to give up the idee of the attack. We coulda taken the guns with a little trouble—gettin' horses to drive 'em out—or we coulda prepared to stand and do battle. But I guess Captain figgered this was the least trouble, and fixed it just as good."

It was clear that Grandpa had an eager, attentive audience at last, and he was making the most of it. "Now layin' there on the floor afore the robbers even got started for the bank, it came to me the only chance of outwittin' 'em was to fix the wagon wheels the way we

164

fixed those gun carriages. I didn't want 'em runnin' around town, shootin' up innocent people, so I figgered to loosen the wheel nuts just enough so they'd get outa town. The wheels would come off on the curve of Morgan's Hill. Reuben did what I told him, and it happened just the right way."

Grandpa took a drink of coffee and went on sagely. "It were a good thing I had that experience in memory, now, weren't it? And what a good thing I had Reuben to carry out my orders! He went beyond 'em, of course, to run down the street and get Central started givin' the alarm. It was for love of me, and it shows how brave the boy is. . . ."

Grandpa's voice had trailed off and Reuben was sure he was close to tears again. Everything was silent for a few moments except for the sounds of eating, then Grandpa blew his nose loudly and went on, "I had to burn him bad to free his hands and he never once whimpered. That were a hard thing to do. I worry

165

now 'bout how long they'll be hurtin' him. . . ."
Grandpa stopped talking, having said everything he had to say.

Papa spoke heartily. "No need to worry about the burns. The doctor says they're not deep and will heal nicely with time. Reuben will probably be fine when he wakes up. Burns are not usually painful after the first hours, I'm told."

Reuben looked down at his hands. For some time, while listening to the absorbing conversation, he had almost forgotten about them. In their heavy bandages they looked like the hands of a boxer. Papa was right—he felt no pain any more, only a dull throbbing.

There was a pause again, and then Papa went on: "It was real fine of both of you—using your heads that way. Of course, you never should have been on the road so late, but we can overlook that now since all turned out well. Just think, Constable"—there was real pride in his voice—"an old man and a boy not

166

yet twelve managed to outwit the meanest pair of bandits in three states!"

The constable chuckled hugely. "Indeed, it is that—a fine thing! And a for-rtunate one," he went on heartily. "They'll be doing no more jobs now, those two! We had 'em, Sher-riff and I, like rats in a hole there at the bottom of Mor-rgan's Hill. 'Twas a sight, I can tell you! We came on them, both of us, about the same time. He, coming by auto, made it from Still-water-r as fast as I from town, what with hitching up and all. There was your-r team, walking ar-round all confused, pulling the empty wagon with two wheels off, and the two men lying in the ditch stunned like. They har-rdly knew what had happened to them, except that each had a busted ar-rm."

Papa spoke cheerfully. "Ah, well, broken bones will mend. And a long spell in prison will give them time to think things over. It's not too late for them to mend their ways and become decent, law-abiding men again."

"Let's hope so," said the constable. He was not through with the story of the capture. Now it was his turn to have an attentive audience.

"So we puts them under-r ar-rest, you know, and takes them to the automobile, and they gets to r-ride to jail in a fine new machine, big as you please. I said to Sher-riff, it's tr-reating 'em too good! But they'll stand tr-rial in good time and you'll be called to testify—you and the boy. It's a good thing to know they'll not be making any mor-re tr-rouble."

Reuben got up from the floor and began to dress. It went slowly and awkwardly, for he had to use the tips of his fingers, all that showed of his hands under the bandages. He was strangely light-headed, and his legs felt heavy and numb. He had to sit down on the bed for a few minutes before he felt able to walk downstairs.

At the doorway of the dining room he stopped, clearing his throat. He felt suddenly bashful and could think of no other way to let them know that he was there.

Everyone turned to look at him. "Are the horses all right?" he asked. It was the first thing that came into his head to say.

Then he immediately became so completely the center of attention that he was embarrassed. Mama quickly made a place for him at the table, patting his head lovingly as she ran back and forth with the dishes. Papa gave him one of his rare smiles, and even Will and Johnny looked at him with new interest.

"The horses are back, strong and frisky as ever," said Papa. "You don't need to worry about them, but how do you feel, Son?"

Without even waiting for an answer, he went on, "When I told you and Grandpa here to take care of each other, I didn't realize what it would mean. But I guess you both did just that—from the beginning of the trip right up to that business with the bandits in Marine!"

Grandpa had pushed back his chair, and

now he stood up and came over to where Reuben sat. He put both his hands on Reuben's shoulders. "Here's our hero," he said. "It was this boy, a-doin' what I told him, that made my plan work. He didn't ever let me down. He even risked his life to make sure nothin' happened to me."

Tears were near the surface again in Grandpa's voice. He turned quickly and stumped back to his chair. He began eating hurriedly. For once he had been able to finish everything he had to say.

Reuben found it easy to speak now. "No, it was Grandpa's plan that was the important thing. I couldn't have thought of anything as good as that by myself."

With Mama's help, and using the tips of his fingers to hold the spoon, he was able to begin eating. He swallowed a few mouthfuls. "It was because of Grandpa that I wasn't scared," he said, swaggering a bit. "I knew he would outsmart those bandits, if anyone could!"

Some day he might reveal how pitiful and weak Grandpa had looked stumping into the blacksmith shop with the revolver at his back. He might even admit—perhaps to Mama some time—how fearful he had been of coming back and finding Grandpa beaten, or worse, on the smithy floor. But there was no need for such revelations now. This was a day for celebrating victory.

Constable Campbell seemed to be the only one doing full justice to Mama's good dinner of ham and cream gravy and corn pudding. Everyone else seemed more interested in hearing all the details of the robbery and capture of the bandits. Reuben was glad that his sisters, at least, were in school or they would have kept asking questions and pouring out admiration until he would not have been able to stand it. Even Will, usually so superior because of his age, was full of approval today.

"It does seem as if the epidemic of bank robberies should soon be over," Papa was saying, eating his raisin tapioca with relish. "It's lasted too long, this lawlessness, and much of it started right here in Minnesota with those James boys. Let's hope the time of bank robberies and other lawlessness will soon be ending."

"And that's the tr-ruth!" echoed the constable piously. He touched the silver badge on his chest, as if to reassure himself that he had a direct responsibility in assuring that ending.

10

Grandpa Prepares A Speech

Reuben's hands began to heal rapidly. He was even able to go back to school on the following day, but he purposely waited to arrive until just before the bell began to ring. He took his seat quietly amid excited whispers. He hoped no fuss would be made over him, but he had not counted on Miss Hibbard.

After the opening song each morning she always gave a little talk about Manners and Morals. The children listened attentively, grateful for anything that postponed the day's arithmetic lessons.

On this particular day, she had written the word "Courage" in large letters on the front blackboard, so that even the smallest pupils should be able to see what it looked like. She pointed to each letter in turn with the pointer, spelling it out slowly.

"Courage is a special kind of bravery," she began carefully. "We might say that it's the kind of bravery that gets things done in dangerous circumstances, when there isn't much time even to think. . . ."

She went on to explain that now she was using Reuben, their schoolmate, as an example of courage. She pictured the scene in the dark blacksmith shop, with the bandits in power, and the old man and boy at first so frightened and helpless. Then she went on to tell of the courage shown by both of them in risking pain and danger to follow a plan that would foil the plans of the lawless men. She talked with such dramatic power that every one of the children, right down to the littlest first grader, sat listening, perfectly still.

As she continued, one by one, they began turning around to stare at Reuben with such fascination that he grew red and began to squirm. He wished something might happen to end the embarrassment he was feeling. And she didn't know the full story either.

Miss Hibbard finally had to pause for breath. In the sudden silence he spoke up, almost without thinking. "I wish you'd stop

talking about me! It was Grandpa was the hero anyway—not me. I couldn't have thought up a plan like that; I was just about scared stiff. I haven't told that before, but it's true. Just 'cause Grandpa's old and talks a lot about the war and such, he's treated like a silly old fool most of the time. They make him feel he's no good for anything any more. But he's awful smart in all kinds of ways. I've always known that; that's why I was willing to follow his orders without really knowing what he had in mind, what he was planning to do. I guess he's showed everybody a few things!"

As suddenly as he had spoken Reuben fell silent. He stopped and looked down at his desk, surprised and embarrassed at his unusual outburst. Even Miss Hibbard seemed at a loss for words.

"Well!" she said at last. "That was quite a speech, Reuben! But let's watch our grammar. It's 'shown' not 'showed' — and I'm sure you remember I've pointed out many times that 'awful' means 'full of awe or terror,' and that hardly describes your grandfather's cleverness, now does it? You meant 'very,' I'm sure."

"Yes, ma'am," said Reuben, subsiding. He began fussing with the pencil box inside his desk, anxious to get to work and put an end to the talking.

"Well, so much for that," said Miss Hibbard briskly. "You may turn to your arithmetic examples now and begin working them. Numbers on the blackboard for the first, second, and third grades. I'll give out the pages for the others."

But it was a different story at noon. It was Thursday, the next to the last day of Reuben's stay-in recesses. After eating lunch, he took his seat as usual. He did not mind staying in today, because, of course, he could not play baseball with bandaged hands anyway. He opened his book to the story he had been reading three days ago.

But Miss Hibbard seemed in a mood for

178

talking. She asked how his hands and wrists felt, and how he managed to do such things as dress himself and eat his meals with the big bandages on. Then she asked him what had been his thoughts when the masked men approached him that frightening evening. He answered as truthfully as he could.

Then she began to ask him all sorts of questions about Grandpa. What about his service in the war? And what about his knowing General Sherman? She was kind and admiring, and she had the family relationship completely straightened out now.

She paused a moment and cleared her throat. She seemed uncertain exactly how to go on—how to say what was on her mind.

"You know," she said tentatively, "we'll soon be having our closing day program and picnic. After this heroic adventure of yours and your grandfather's—well, I've been wondering. Why couldn't we have our program on the 30th? They call that day Decoration

Day here. Back East, we call it Memorial Day
and it's an important holiday in memory of
the men who fell in battle. Here in the Mid-
west it doesn't really seem to be properly observed, I've gathered. That's why I'd like to
get the custom started—at least in this community. Why couldn't we put on a real Memorial Day program in connection with our
closing day picnic? It seems now I've thought
of it, I can't get the idea out of my head."

Reuben waited a bit impatiently, for he
wanted to get back to his book. But Miss
Hibbard had more to say.

"I've been thinking," she went on, "if we
had this Memorial Day program, I'd like to
have your grandfather as the main speaker.
He's the logical one, really — a Union army
veteran living right here in this community.
Do you think he'd be willing to make a
speech?"

Reuben was almost overcome with surprise.
He could not remember that such an invita-

tion had ever come to Grandpa before. It would make him ever so proud. He would know now at last that he had real importance, in the way in which he wanted to be important —as a Union army veteran.

Reuben flushed. "Oh, yes," he said eagerly. "Grandpa could give a fine speech! He explains the war better to me than any history book. He talks so different about it—I mean it doesn't seem so dead and far away as it does in the books."

Then, remembering his stubbornness about the Arbor Day program, he stammered a bit, trying to think what to say. He blurted out earnestly, "If you want me to, I'll—I mean if you wanted me to speak a piece now, I'd be glad to do it. I wouldn't be—well, it wouldn't be like when you asked me to speak that poem for the Arbor Day program." He stopped in confusion and looked out the window.

Miss Hibbard smiled kindly. "I'm very glad to hear it," she said. "But I don't think we'll

181

be needing any recitations for this program. We'll be wanting some music, and maybe some marching or a drill or something, but otherwise the speech will be enough. With final examinations coming up, there isn't really time to prepare for a big program now. Of course, we might sing a song like 'Battle Hymn of the Republic' and you could play your cornet for the singing. I think that would make a fine Memorial Day program!"

That was the way the first planning was done. It was agreed that Reuben would ask Grandpa if he would make the speech, to give remembrances of his war experiences and to "bring in some patriotic thoughts," as Miss Hibbard put it.

"It's the spirit of the thing that's important," she said. "I just can't think of anything more suitable than what we've planned. But tell your grandfather to limit his speech to half an hour or so. It shouldn't be much longer anyway. It's hard to keep children quiet for long speeches, especially when they're getting hungry and know that a picnic dinner is waiting."

It was this last that made Reuben begin to worry. All too well he remembered Grandpa's weakness for long talk, especially when he got on the subject of the war. "Old Sven's long-winded war spiels" had become almost a joke everywhere. Even Papa and Mama sometimes laughed about it to each other when they thought no one heard them. Like everyone else, they sometimes failed to hear him out when he got sort of long-winded.

Reuben wondered if, in spite of the way everyone admired Grandpa's recent heroism, the same thing that happened at the last Fourth of July picnic might not happen again. Then it had been old Colonel Wilkinson of Stillwater standing on the platform, trying to make himself heard while people whispered to each other, began to eat their lunches, or even walked away. After a while he had just

stopped and sat down, and Reuben still remembered the look on his face. If they could
act like that on the Fourth—to a man who had
been a colonel in the Union army — Reuben
found himself shivering with dread. This
could turn into a very sad experience for
Grandpa. It could spoil all the good things
he'd been hearing since the bank robbery.

Grandpa, of course, agreed enthusiastically
to Miss Hibbard's request. He seemed to think
it quite natural that he should be the one
chosen to speak at this kind of program. "I
have plenty to tell," he said enthusiastically.

Since the Stillwater trip, it seemed that
Papa regarded Reuben differently. He showed
that he depended on him more and even entrusted him with important tasks now and
then. Sometimes they worked together at
something, and Reuben discovered at such
times that he could talk to Papa more easily
and ask him about things that bothered him.

One day when they were putting up a new

calf pen in the barn, Reuben asked what he thought about Grandpa making the speech. Papa looked thoughtful. "I expect he knows more about the war and the building of this country than anybody hereabouts," he said. "He *should* be the one to speak about it. We owe him that bit of honor, but I guess we never would have thought of it, if it hadn't been for Miss Hibbard."

This should have satisfied Reuben, but as the days went by and everyone at school began talking excitedly about the program and picnic, Reuben almost wished Miss Hibbard had never had the idea. He could not help vaguely dreading the day.

At his mother's suggestion, he was trying to help Grandpa with the preparation of the speech. That way, she pointed out, he would be able to make sure that it was what Miss Hibbard wanted. But in these sessions Grandpa kept bringing up one story after another that he felt must be included. Reuben's uneasiness grew. The speech would last for hours!

They practiced out in the orchard after school. Again and again Reuben explained how the program was arranged, how much time was allotted to each part. He tried to get Grandpa to plan exactly what to say.

"Tell a couple of good stories, you know— things that happened on the march. Then about the Union being preserved and the slaves freed — things like that. Most of the speeches I've heard on the Fourth of July seem to go that way. Only, being it's Memorial Day, you should say something about honoring those who died for their country, too. That's the way Miss Hibbard explained it to me, anyway."

Reuben paused for breath and looked up earnestly into Grandpa's face. "It can be ever so much better than a Fourth of July speech, I think—if it goes right." He was trying to re-assure himself as well as Grandpa.

186

"Oh, I've got plenty to say!" Grandpa laid his pipe in the crotch of a young apple tree and placed himself firmly in front of Reuben as if facing an audience. "Don't worry. And if it's stories I should begin with, why, I've sure got all kinds of them! Mebbe I should tell about the time I was posted to guard the well at this big plantation. We'd seen the lady run from the house, put her silver in the bucket an' lower it down the well. She didn't know, of course, that those of us up ahead caught the shine of the silver in the sun as we came down the road. We knowed what she were up to. But Gus put me on guard at that well, just so no one would get the idee he had to have a drink from that one special old oaken bucket. I kept 'em all away," he chortled, "by sayin' the water had been poisoned by the Rebs!

"And, of course, I'll want to tell 'bout how I went along when the telegram was sent to President Lincoln — the one told him that Savannah was ours, taken without trouble. I copied the words off the paper—the one Uncle Billy's aide had to write from—right there in the telegraph office. I still have it somewheres, I know. Let's see now, where is that little paper? I do hope I haven't lost it—I've had it with me so long."

He rummaged through an assortment of folded papers at the bottom of his money pouch. "Well, no matter," he said at last. "I think I remember what it said, anyway. It went like this: 'I beg to present as a Christmas present to you the city of Savannah' and it was signed 'William T. Sherman.'"

Grandpa stood silent, completely lost in the past. The soft May breeze lifted his straggling white locks. His eyes seemed veiled to the present time and place, as if seeing altogether different scenes. Reuben coughed to bring him back to the present again. Grandpa looked down at him slowly.

"Yes sir," he said, collecting himself briskly. "That was it—and mebbe a few more words

188

I don't exactly recall. But I never fergit the main part. I were there!" He held himself proudly erect. "But say, you ain't catching cold? I heard you cough just now. I've warned you 'bout going barefoot in wet grass."

Reuben reassured him hastily. "I can tell you — just about, anyway — what President Lincoln said in the message he sent back to Sherman," he added with a touch of scholarly pride. "It's not in the history books at all; Miss Hibbard told it to us. She knows extra little things like that — that's what makes her so good in history. Well, President Lincoln telegraphed back to General Sherman and asked him to express his, the President's, thanks to all his men. I bet you didn't know you'd been thanked by Abraham Lincoln!"

"Have I, now?" said Grandpa with pleased surprise. "Now ain't it a good thing you have a teacher like that? I'd never knowed it otherwise. You see, on account of I had to go into hospital for a while in Savannah, I likely

190

missed that bit of news. Well, I guess I won't mention that in my speech, though. It might sound a bit like I was braggin'.

"But one more thing I would like to tell—about the little colored boy who wouldn't leave with the others, but stayed behind to take care of his sick dog. Oh, that were pure pitiful to see—both of 'em so weak and hungry! Have I told you 'bout that—how we came on 'em, and what we did?"

"Yes, you have," said Reuben patiently, "and it's an awfully good story, but you see there won't be time for you to tell everything like that. Miss Hibbard said you were only to talk for half an hour. You will just have to leave out some things. You know how kids get—and grownups too—when they're hungry and it gets close to noontime. They get restless and only think about eating."

Grandpa looked downcast, so Reuben hastened to add, "But if anyone can make 'em sit up and listen, you can, Grandpa! All you've

191

got to do is make them understand a little bit what the war was like—and what it was about. And make them remember those who died. And then you'll be through. You can sit down and rest."

The bandages finally came off the burned hands and Reuben was able to play the cornet again. He began practicing "The Battle Hymn of the Republic," even though he had played it before. He must know it extra well now. Each day at school the children practiced singing and marching around the space where the platform was to be set up. Reuben and the flag-bearer walked in front—"not exactly the way an army marches" according to Miss Hibbard, "but close enough to suggest it in a general way."

"Your part is a sort of grand finale after the speech, so you must learn to sing in tune and march in time. Now once more. One, two— one, two—" They marched and marched and sang and sang, and somehow they did not get tired of all the practicing. It was something new and different in a program, and they were eager to have a share in making it a success.

But even as he marched and blew, Reuben was worrying. He kept thinking, "What if Grandpa talks too long? What if he forgets where he is and keeps going on and on? What if he just stands there, looking off in the distance, the way he does when he goes back in the past? People will begin to talk, and maybe even walk away. And how's he going to feel if they treat him like poor old Colonel Wilkinson last Fourth of July? He'll know what it means, no matter what I say to him afterwards. Even being a hero like he was in Marine — I guess that isn't enough when you're old. People still get impatient if you get the least bit tiresome. They forget all the good things about you."

Reuben finally confided his fears to Mama. She admitted that she had been worrying too.

193

She had been trying to think of something they could do to prevent Grandpa from embarrassment. She had a few ideas that she thought might work.

"With all the attention he's been getting lately, he does seem more spry and alert than he's been in a long time. There really is a difference. But we know his weakness," she went on, in a practical way. "We must prevent him from falling into his usual habit.

"Why wouldn't it be a good idea for you to arrange to give him a signal when it's time to stop? You could tell him beforehand that you're going to—by striking up the first note of your march tune or something. Explain it to Miss Hibbard, and she can give you the sign. She doesn't know Grandpa, but I'm sure she knows what most old men are like."

This idea did not appeal to Reuben. He thought it might embarrass Grandpa even more. He could picture the sheepish look that would come into his face at the blast from the

194

cornet. He could imagine the confusion with which the old man would stop speaking and sit down. It would spoil the triumph of making the speech altogether. He decided that he would say nothing; he would just hope for the best and let things take their course.

Every day, though, he talked to Grandpa about the speech. He kept repeating the time limit—"just half an hour, you know, Grandpa. You don't have to try to tell very much, really. Mostly they just want to have a good look at you because you're sort of a hero now. And you're the only veteran of the Civil War for miles around."

He hoped desperately that this would have the desired effect. He figured that maybe Grandpa would get used to thinking of the speech in terms of briefness and precision.

And Grandpa would answer cheerfully, "Don't you worry, boy! I'm a-goin' to give a real good speech. You won't have cause to feel 'shamed. There's plenty I have to say!"

11

Grandpa Speaks On Memorial Day

And then quite suddenly it was the 30th of May! Folding chairs had been set in rows in the school yard, and women were sitting in them, their full skirts overflowing onto the grass in bright splashes of color. Men and small children sat on the ground beside the chairs, with the school children directly in front of the platform. Reuben and Joe Jonson, the flag-bearer, were in the exact center of the group.

The children whispered excitedly among themselves. There had never been such a crowd at a school program before. The whole yard was overflowing with people, even though it was a weekday. Most of the farmers were still planting corn, and this was a fine, warm day, just right for field work. But here they were, busy farmers and their wives, all dressed up and turned out for the Memorial Day program Miss Hibbard had planned.

A small wooden plank platform had been built the evening before by some of the men. Now it was gaily decorated with flags and bouquets of lilacs and late apple blossoms. The pleasant odors of sawdust and blossoms mingled with the aroma of a few cigars which had been lighted by some of the men. On the platform, with Miss Hibbard and Grandpa, sat the three members of the school board—Mr. Glass, Mr. Lindgren, and Mr. Erickson.

A phonograph, topped with a huge morning-glory horn, had been borrowed from Mr. Glass for use in the singing of "America." He had fussed with it importantly from the moment of his arrival and would allow no one else to touch it. While he was winding it and adjusting the horn, the crowd sat quiet,

197

watching respectfully. This was the only phonograph in the entire school district; it marked the Glasses as the most distinguished music specialists for miles around.

When it was time to begin, Mr. Glass, who was also a member of the church choir, started the music playing and stepped forward to lead. Everyone rose to sing "America" to the accompaniment of the recorded brass band. The music floated out bravely, though somewhat faintly, and with certain odd crackling sounds. The sharp tenor of Mr. Glass could be heard even above the voices of the children, but when he occasionally faltered on the words, it was the children's voices that carried through triumphantly.

Reuben kept his eyes fixed on Miss Hibbard as they sat down. She was going to introduce Grandpa for his speech, and somehow he hoped that the words she said would make Grandpa remember about not talking too long. She looked unusually nice, with her heavy golden hair piled high in a coronet braid and topped with a big black velvet bow. Her white lawn dress, daintily sprigged with pink roses and tied with a pink ribbon sash, had brought gasps of admiration from the girls.

She came forward now and spoke a few words of welcome to the expectant crowd. At first her voice was low and hesitant so that it could scarcely be heard. But as she went on to explain the meaning of Memorial Day, it grew stronger. A note of pride came through. She was pleased and proud that she, a complete stranger here last fall, had been able to bring this large crowd together for a patriotic observance on a busy spring day. She began to talk of Grandpa, calling him "a veteran of the glorious Union army who had served with distinction in the ranks under General Sherman." Then she went on to speak of his and Reuben's "heroic action in recently helping to capture a dangerous pair of bandits in a neighboring town."

199

She closed the graceful introduction with the words: "I thought it most fitting that this Memorial Day program, which is also our closing day of school, should have as chief speaker, Corporal Sven Anderson. He is one of the last of 'the old boys in blue' and will tell us some of his war experiences and bring the message of the day."

Reuben's mouth was suddenly dry, and he swallowed hard. He felt a sudden great compassion for Grandpa, well remembering what a frightening thing it could be to face a crowd of staring eyes, for he had been on a few school programs himself.

Grandpa moved forward stiffly. He was wearing his one good suit, a somewhat shiny black serge. His starched white shirt billowed out in front, giving him an unnaturally big chest. Mama had tied a narrow black tie into a neat bow at his throat. It looked small and almost lost on the creaking stiffness of the vast white shirt front.

His white hair fringe stuck out in spiky points from under the faded blue army cap. Like many other returned soldiers, he had worn out the coat and trousers years ago as farm clothes. But somehow the cap alone managed to give him a certain important dignity. He looked exactly like what he was—an old Civil War soldier.

Reuben had tried not to stare at him so hard as the others. Now, glancing up at him as he stood ready to speak, he felt a great rush of pride. He looked around at his schoolmates with flashing eyes. This was not just any old grandpa! This was Corporal Sven Anderson, of the Fourth Minnesota—and the Grand Army of the Republic! This was one of General Sherman's "hand-picked army of 60,000 men." You couldn't take that away from him; it was in all the history books that Sherman had called them that. For a few moments all Reuben's worries about the speech disappeared.

Grandpa removed his cap. He stood for a

202

few moments squeezing it in his hand. The light applause died down, and everyone waited expectantly. He cleared his throat and then, almost apologetically, he began to speak.

"I guess you all know me better as 'old Sven by Sunfish Lake,'" he began, smiling shyly. "Many of you weren't even born forty years ago when the war ended, but you've heard me tell more'n once, I expect, 'bout happenings in that war. Last thing I expected when I came to this country was that I'd be conscripted for the army; we had that in the old country and I didn't like it. But I was, and I went in the army from Fort Snelling. I had to leave just at harvest time to become a soldier with Sherman. I guess you know, too, that I'd paid my three hunded dollars for a substitute to go in my place, so's I shouldn't have to go. Havin' a family and a new farm to tend, it didn't seem as how I ought to go away to war. You know 'bout that too." He stood uncertainly, as if trying to think what else to say.

He cleared his throat again. "But the war didn't end in a year or two as everyone expected. The Union kept needin' more men, and so my name came up again in the draft. And this time I didn't have the three hundred dollars to pay for someone to go in my place. I had to be conscripted into the army. That's how I got into the war and was with Sherman in his last campaign and march.

"I could cert'nly tell you some fine stories! He were the finest gen'ral in our country's history, you know! And we had some experiences in that campaign I never fergit. But you might find it a mite long if I got started talkin' on that, and I don't aim to make a long speech. You can ask me afterwards 'bout anything you want to know; I'm allus glad to talk. You know that too." He smiled again.

Reuben's heart was in his throat. It seemed to be going all right so far—nothing special, just a kind of rambling on. But everyone seemed interested. Reuben hoped, though, that he would remember to say a few things about patriotism and honor to our dead and all that, because that was what Memorial Day was about.

Grandpa was still smiling. A light titter had swept over the audience at his last words. "He's showing them that he can take a joke about himself at least," Reuben thought. "They like that."

But suddenly the old man grew serious. He looked earnestly into the sea of faces and began talking fast.

"I've been glad all my life—long as I had to go to war—that I had the good fortune to serve under such a man as General Sherman. He knew what war meant—and he didn't like it! He was a great gen'ral but he hated fightin' and bloodshed. You know what he said once: 'War is h—, er, a turrible thing!' "

Reuben shuddered with relief. Grandpa had almost said the bad word, the one only preachers were supposed to say when they talked about where you went if you'd been bad. It was exactly the word General Sherman had used—Miss Hibbard had told him that in one of their conversations, outside of class, of course. It showed how awful he thought war was, because you didn't use that word in ordinary ways of talking.

Grandpa was really fired up now. "Uncle Billy said the only way to stop wars is for everyone to understand what a bad thing it is to let 'em get started. I mind what he said one evenin' when he talked to a big crowd of us—our own division and some others. He said anyone who starts trouble, like the South did, has to be shown how wrong it was, even if it hurts 'em some at the time. His words as I remember were: 'I regret the bitter feelings we are making, though they are to be expected. But those who struck the first blow made this war necessary. They reproach us now, but the day will come when they will thank us.'"

Reuben felt little shivers running through his scalp, which was a sure sign that what he was hearing had the power to thrill and inspire. But now Grandpa stood quiet, completely lost in memory. He might have been standing again beside a Georgia campfire, listening to his leader.

He stood still so long that the audience, which had been so attentive, began to stir. Men glanced meaningfully at each other. Two small boys near the platform began to push each other playfully. The watching children tittered, wondering what they would do next. Some of the audience watched the old man; some looked away in embarrassment. Quite plainly his mind was wandering. It began to look as if he were really not up to this, after all.

Reuben kept his eyes fixed on Grandpa hopefully. He had always been able to recall him to the present, by a movement or a word, or even a cough. But what could he do now, sitting here in a crowd of people?

207

"I've got to make him look at me—I've got to!" Almost without thinking, he let out a great wracking cough, the kind that usually made Grandpa look at him and say reprovingly "Catchin' cold, ain't you?" or "Too early to go barefoot," or "Ought to have your under-woolies on."

But there was no response from Grandpa now. He still seemed very far away.

Then Reuben lifted his cornet ever so slightly until the bright gleaming brass caught the sunlight and blazed like a small sun right into Grandpa's eyes. The brooding look vanished and a quick upward glance took its place, and then the old eyes looked straight down into Reuben's anxious ones. A quick look of understanding passed between them. Grandpa pushed at his billowing shirt front and took a step forward.

"But I see the sun is almost directly overhead—must be it's gettin' close to dinnertime. I reckon you're all mighty hungry by this time.

And you want to hear the children sing and see them march. I'm a-goin' to sit down in just a minute. I only want to show them — the children—how we was greeted when we marched through Georgia. We was singin' then, too, you know, mostly to keep from feelin' so tired and so lonesome for our home folks, and the new-free colored folk came from miles around to watch us march by and foller along after if they could. They stood by the roadsides or sat on fences or shanty doorsteps, and allus they took off their caps or aprons and waved and waved as we came by. . . ."

Grandpa raised his right arm, holding his cap aloft, while his face shone with youth and fervor. The audience sat watching in rapt amazement at the scene he re-created.

"They shouted to us, and they called greetings, and joined in our singin'! And they cried, 'Hurrah for General Sherman and his men! Hurrah! Hurrah!' "

Grandpa's arms dropped to his sides and he

stood still. "I never fergit it," he said simply. "And I never fergit either the brave comrades who marched beside me—those who fell in battle, and those who still live. Many are gone. May they live forever in memory."

He turned suddenly and sat down. Reuben could tell that Grandpa was close to tears again—but so were many others! There were tears in his own eyes. He didn't care!

What a fine, dignified figure Grandpa made as he sat there on the platform, shaking hands with Mr. Erickson, Mr. Lindgren, and Mr. Glass! Now and then he wiped his eyes with his cap, unable to find the handkerchief in his pocket.

Miss Hibbard was wiping her eyes too, with a tiny, lacy handkerchief, but she managed to look straight at Reuben and smile brightly. It was plain that she was tremendously pleased with the speech.

Now the audience was standing, clapping hands loudly. Some of the women waved their handkerchiefs. Grandpa stood up once and made a slight bow, and then they clapped even harder.

After a while Miss Hibbard rose and came forward, giving the signal for the march to begin. Reuben stood up, the flag-bearer took his place beside him, and the first notes of the cornet came out full and clear. The children fell into their places in line and began to sing, and the line moved out slowly in front of the watching crowd.

Reuben stepped along proudly beside Joe, who being the tallest boy in school, was able to carry the flag like a real soldier. The other children followed briskly behind, singing out loudly: "Mine eyes have seen the glory of the coming of the Lord. . . ."

The strong rhythm of the song kept their feet in step as they marched. After all the hours of practice there was no faltering or straggling. They seemed caught up in the spirit of Grandpa's inspired finish. They thrilled to the idea

211

of marching and singing like the Union army had done under Sherman, with Grandpa one of the soldiers.

It seemed to Reuben that all his worry for Grandpa must end forever with this day. His grandfather had come into his own at last. All around him people were smiling warmly and saying fine, praising words: "A great speech! A fine program! We're proud of our grand old soldier!" Could anyone ever again forget what Grandpa had been—and still was?

When they came to the chorus, Reuben wished he could stop playing just long enough to join in the singing. He, too, wanted to sing and shout: "Glory, glory, hallelujah!"

Everything had turned out fine—even gloriously! It was *his* Grandpa they were talking about—his grand Grandpa!

THE END

About the Author

The compassionate feelings and intense convictions of Mrs. Christgau's story are those of her childhood, expressed with the perspectives and skills of a mature and able writer. Perhaps this is why this book communicates so directly to present-day children who, more than ever before are exploring relationships with old people—grandparents and great-grandparents.

Like old Sven in her story, Mrs. Christgau's grandfather needed respect from a family too busy to allow him the frailties and garrulity that come with old age.

A mother of three grown children, Mrs. Christgau has had considerable teaching experience in addition to her professional writing. She is President of the Association of University Women in Oakland, California, where she and her husband now live.

About the Artist

Leo Ramon Summers was born in Los Angeles, California, and raised in Seattle, Washington where he attended the Bernly School of Art. His active career in art began in Chicago as a free-lance artist for the Ziff-Davis Publishing Company. In 1954, Mr. Summers resigned from Ziff-Davis to establish his own studio in New York City.

His work has appeared in most of the leading magazines, and he has been published by more than a dozen major publishing houses.

Mr. Summers is unusual in that, while he does intensive reading and research, he does not draw from photographs, models or sketches. Today, drawing from memory is a lost art; he practices it and the results are a highly individual style of pen and ink drawings.